DANIEL'S FIRE

Not once since my injury have I shown a woman my scars. Not any of the three whole dates I've been on. None of them made me feel the way Camille makes me feel....

DANIEL'S FIRE

Quidell Brothers Book 2

KRIS AUSTEN RADCLIFFE

Six Love Erotic Romance

THE WORLDS OF
KRIS AUSTEN RADCLIFFE

HOT CONTEMPORARY ROMANCE
THE QUIDELL BROTHERS

Thomas's Muse
Daniel's Fire
Robert's Soul
Thomas's Need
Andrew's Kiss (*coming soon*)

DANIEL'S FIRE

A Quidell Brothers ROMANCE

By
Kris Austen Radcliffe

Six Love Erotic Romance
Minneapolis

www.krisaustenradcliffe.com

Second print edition, June 2018
Version: 6.25.2018
ISBN: 978-1-939730-60-2

DANIEL'S FIRE

A Quidell Brothers
ROMANCE

CHAPTER 1

Daniel

My truck's service indicator winks on as I pull into the lot of my son's daycare. Frowning, I park outside the big Community Center building and stare at the little blue wrench and the letter-number combo on my dash. It's one of the expensive service reminders. One involving every filter and hose attached to my truck's engine, and from my last check, it probably means new tires as well.

I pull the key and sit back, mentally adding "take in the truck" to the cloud of nag inside my head. Most people would call it a mental to-do list. To me, it's a massing zombie scene: I'm on the rooftop and each time I tick something off the list, I get an undead kill shot.

Most days, I get more of them than they get bites out of me.

It's a violent way to keep a to-do list, I know. But visualization is one of the techniques they taught me while I laid on my back in that damned hospital recovering after the doctors inserted pins into my shoulder. And my thigh. And layered on the skin grafts. My doc told me if popping the heads off slow, lumbering zombies helps decrease my stress level, then by all means I should pop away.

Both my brothers think it's hilarious. Some guys have stacks of porn on the top shelves of their bedroom closets. I have stacks of shitty movies because my little brother Rob buys every idiotic zombie DVD he finds.

I glance up at the wide steel and concrete expanse of the Community Center's boxlike, early nineties architecture. My kid's in there right now, laughing and playing with the other four-year-olds, and I can't help but think that I need to up my game. Life's got too many shitty zombies. I have a boy to protect.

I look at the sun, feeling its warmth for a second, and breathe in. The air smells fresh, though the highway is on the other side of the hill and the road noise hums through the lot. A summer breeze blows and the occasional cloud keeps it from getting too hot. It's a nice day.

I count, because it's another technique the doc at the hospital taught me. To understand the moment. To see what's really here. And to live.

Sometimes it's hard. But I do it. I have a kid.

Bart's daycare teacher—the amazing Ms. Cunningham, who used to teach high school English before "retiring" to organize and run the community-based daycare—set up a strawberry picking field trip for all the kids at the Center. She called me personally, claiming I was one of her favorite students back in the day, and asked if I would like to come along.

Who am I to say no to Ms. Cunningham? Besides, I get to spend time with my kid *and* watch the pretty young teachers sticking out their sweet round asses while they bend over to pick berries.

I may not have stacks of porn in my closet, but I'm still a man. Even if my scars and my life have shut down dating.

I slam the truck door and lean against the front fender, stretching my hamstring. I changed into cargo shorts and a long-sleeved t-shirt before driving over. At the time, I didn't notice that the scar on my leg was visible.

My brothers tell me not to be so self-conscious. But, like seeing what's really here, sometimes it's hard.

I walk toward the Community Center door. The aches are bad

today, even with the nice weather. Maybe the flavor of fresh berries on the tongue and the laughter of little kids will ease at least some of it.

I can hope.

Camille

FORTY PRE-KINDERGARTENERS, SIX TEACHERS AND AIDES, AND EIGHT parents. That's three kids per adult. I hand over a bright green t-shirt and the corresponding green kids' shirts to Ms. Selby, the pregnant parent standing in front of my table, in the middle of the Community Center lobby. She's pretty. Wearing designer yoga maternity wear, too. Her perfume smells like an expensive field of handcrafted French lavender. Or how I imagine a field of expensive Old World lavender tended only by the most artisanal hands would smell. The closest I'll ever get to France is downloaded movies and the occasional glass of fine wine.

"I'm supposed to put this on?" Smiling, though she's obviously annoyed by the chaotic green of the shirt, she holds it like she would a pair of stinky workout shoes.

"It's so your group can easily identify you. And you, them." I point to the three little kid shirts and her assigned list before pointing toward the room she's with.

Nodding, she takes the shirts and walks down the hall, her designer sandals snapping against the floor.

I watch her go. Sandy—Ms. Cunningham to all the parents—is wrangling her room of little ones, as are the other teachers. I don't get my own room until next week—I'm teaching pull-out art classes—so I'm wrangling the parents.

When I hear the Community Center's door whoosh open I look up, expecting another neighborhood mom to saunter in, or the second dad. We have two today. The first guy, a tech from one of the local computer businesses, walked in early, blinking like he'd never seen the sun before, and went about following directions as well as the best of our students. He waits now in his bright yellow t-shirt in his daughter's room helping the other kids with theirs.

The second one is little Bart's father. Sandy's eyebrow arched just a tad bit when she said his name, and her lips rounded for a fraction of a second. The man has a reputation—a *good* reputation.

I remember the news reports. How Bart's father and another firefighter got a family out of an apartment building before it collapsed. How they'd both been injured. Dan Quidell is a hero.

I've seen Bart's file. Hell, all the teachers have seen his file. We need to know when kids have non-custodial parents who might cause problems and sadly, little Bart is one such kid. So I know what his dad looks like, as I do his ex-wife. Her photo in the file is a six year old snapshot. His, a slightly blurry cell phone snap. Mr. Quidell holds Bart but he's turning away, like he doesn't want his photo taken. Bart, though, is mugging for the photographer, as Bart tends to do.

There'd been the snickers in the break room this morning when Sandy went over the parent list. "Hug a Teacher" mugs held high and the calls to make sure that when Dan Quidell changes into his neon colored parent t-shirt, he does it out in the open, where they all can see.

I rolled my eyes. Because, I'm sure, the man *likes* being considered a piece of meat. The disrespect left a sour taste.

But when the Community Center doors whoosh open and the road noise rolls in, when I see one Mr. Daniel Quidell in the flesh for the first time, only two words echo through my head. Two very unteacher-like words. Two words that sum up the halting physical grace before me: *Holy fuck.*

The sun backlights his body, so I can't immediately see his face, but I see his shape. Like a lot of tall men, he does the slight head duck as he walks across the threshold into the main lobby, even though he has plenty of clearance. He twists too, angling in one broad shoulder before the other.

He moves like the dancers I used to date, gliding on strong, sure legs. But I see the snagging of his joints, and, I suspect, some aches, and I'm sure not all his injuries healed right.

His scars from his firefighter days must still cause him pain.

Stopping just inside the door, under the full glory of the lobby's huge skylight, he curls one sculpted bicep as he reaches to pull off his sunglasses.

The tingle doesn't creep up from my belly or between my legs or from any other part of my body. It manifests from every one of my cells as if I'm standing between two static electricity generators. Two of those huge sparking monstrosities from old movies, the ones Dr. Frankenstein used to bring his monster to life.

I look at the big, gorgeous man framed by the Community Center's entrance, at his well-proportioned chest and arms, his flat abs and his strong, centered-though-pained gait as he walks toward me, and my entire body suddenly has a mind of its own. Or half a mind. It most certainly has *desire*.

Holy fuck bounces through my head again. I want to rub those shoulders. Soothe those aches. Stretch and loosen that body. I want to give him relief in *every* way possible.

He hooks one temple of his sunglasses over the collar of his long-sleeved t-shirt as he glances around. A smile appears as he notices my table. And me.

I hope I'm not blushing. God, I feel like I'm blushing. My skin feels hot and my nipples tingle and I swear if he asks, I'll sneak off to a supply closet with him just so I can suck him off.

Which is unprofessional of me. *Very* unprofessional. For goodness sake, I teach his little boy.

But the smiling Mr. Quidell, with his short chocolate brown hair and his incredible blue-green eyes, is beyond gorgeous.

He extends his hand. "Dan Quidell," he says, his voice washing over me in a wave of warm, deep tones. Damn it, he sounds as good as he looks.

One side of his mouth curls up higher than the other. Just a little, and it gives him a hint of devilishness. He's got a swashbuckling air to him, but in a leader kind of way, like he's the head pirate.

I inhale and stand up straight, determined to be professional. I will not embarrass myself and I most definitely will not embarrass a parent. I like my new job, even if I need to find a second one to pay my rent and my school loans. Losing the job I have because I'm an idiot is out of the question.

I take his hand, shaking once. His fingers are roughly smooth, with that thicker texture testosterone gives a man's skin, and they engulf mine.

I inhale again.

"Ms. Frasier." He nods toward my name tag and I swear his eyes are lingering on my chest. "You're new?" Oh, his voice really is like sonic velvet.

When he releases my hand, I almost sigh. His gaze does the unconscious dance over my breasts and my hips that straight men's eyes do, and it takes all my effort not to wiggle where I stand.

The man is too damned distracting.

But I think he's trying to be professional, too. Because I'm one of his kid's teachers.

"Started this week." I smile as I pretend to look for his name on the list. "I'll be teaching pull-out art classes as soon as my room is set up."

"Bart will like that."

I look up again. He's still smiling, but now the muscles of his face have taken on a deeper pull. His stance changed, too. I can't put my finger on it, but I'm sure, all the way to my bones, that this man loves his son.

And I want to sigh again, but I don't. I dig through the pile and pull out a neon pink, size medium t-shirt. "I have your t-shirt right here."

No way is it going to fit.

Mr. Quidell laughs when he holds it up. "We match."

He's right. I hadn't thought about it, but the store only had six colors, so there's doubling. Each teacher got a color and Sandy put one parent with most of us.

And I got Mr. Quidell.

I *am* blushing. I must be the same color as our shirts.

He's making a face and yanking on the seams of the shirt, like he's trying to stretch it. "Is this the biggest you have?"

"No one warned me about your big broad shoulders," I blurt out.

Oh hell, I think, and curl my lips into a thin line. I almost slap a hand over my mouth, but that would just make things worse.

He laughs again and that crooked smirk reappears—and my stray thought about vanishing into a supply closet with him for a quickie jumps back into my head.

Why am I thinking this way? I know how to keep my libido in check. I'm not some young freshman with a crush on the senior quarterback. Or a hero-worshipping fangirl.

The last thing he needs is to think that I'm some firefighter bunny.

His brow crinkles. His gaze drops away and he steps back, holding the t-shirt up between us like a screen. "I'll make do." When he lowers the t-shirt, he's looking down the hall. "Should I go to Bart's room?"

Did I make some unfriendly facial tic? Did he pick up something from my body language? I stiffen, thinking my ogling made him uncomfortable. He's a parent of one of my students. Damn it, I need to be professional.

Kids are so much easier to deal with than men.

I hand him his group's pink t-shirts and his list. "We'll be lining up in a couple of minutes. Will you be riding on the bus with us?"

He glances at the names before answering. "Had an indicator light come on as I was parking, so it looks like it." A frown jumps across his face before he flashes another friendly-but-distant smile.

I make a show of marking my sheet. Dan Quidell nods one more time, watching me for a longer moment than I expected, then walks away, toward his son.

CHAPTER 2

Daniel

We're in the second bus, bouncing down a county road not far out of town. Bart stares out the window, wide eyed, watching the fields go by. The kids are loud and the bus smells more like rotting milk than the old vinyl seats I remember from my time on school buses. The seats are smaller, too. My other two young charges sit in front of us, because, it seems, my "big broad shoulders" take up a lot of room.

One of the kids, a little girl named Emma, occasionally peeks over the top of her seat. She blinks a few times, her eyes big like she wants to ask me something, then she turns around and sits again.

I'm trying to be attentive. I am. But the new teacher with the soulful dark eyes whose name is Ms. Frasier sits two seats up, and right now she's tucking a strand of her glossy, lovely, I-want-to-wrap-my-fingers-in-it black hair behind her ear. It's up in a ponytail or bun or whatever women call that knot they put on the back of their heads, and the nape of her neck is visible.

There's a slight of sheen of sweat on her skin. She glistens.

God damn, Ms. Frasier is *glistening*.

"Daddy, look!" Bart taps my arm and bounces on the seat. "Horses!"

Sure enough, we pass a pasture with three horses gnawing on grass and swishing their tails, and every kid on our side of the bus rushes the windows. I'm surprised we don't roll.

In the seat in front of us, Emma crawls over her little friend, Mandy. "Horsies!" they squeal in unison.

The pretty Ms. Frasier laughs as she lifts the little one next to her onto her lap and points, and I wonder why Bart's mother couldn't be like that. Then I catch myself. Dwelling helps no one.

And I don't even know Ms. Frasier's first name. When she made a hard face in the lobby—that particular way women move their cheeks and lips when they're closing themselves off to talking to a man—I knew I'd better step back.

Not that it matters. Bart's my priority. He was four years ago when I pulled myself up onto my fucking crutches and out of my hospital bed to face my bitch of an ex-wife in that damned courtroom. Thank the Lord for my lawyer—and the support of my station and my family. Bart's safe now.

But I still wish he had a mom.

Bart smiles and bounces again. "Take a picture, Daddy!" He points at the horses. "Please?"

I quickly pull out my phone and snap a few as we pass more horses.

"Let me see!" He grabs my phone and swipes through the photos. "They're blurry." Frowning, his big blue eyes sad, he hands it back.

"Sorry, little man." I tuck the phone into my pocket.

Bart pats my elbow. "That's okay, Daddy. I'll draw a picture so we both remember." He nods once like he *knows* he's taking care of his thick-headed daddy and returns to looking out the window.

Grinning, I muss his hair, and thank the whole wide world for my great kid.

Emma is watching me again. Her little eyes stare over the top of the seat. "Are you a superhero?" she whispers. "You look like a superhero."

Next to her, I hear another little whisper. "Superheroes aren't *real*, Emma! My mommy said so."

Bart beams. I lean close. "What do I say, Doctor Bartman, sir? Do I tell them about our lair? Minion One wants to know."

Emma screeches.

Two seats up, the lovely Ms. Frasier leans over her seat. "Sit down, you two." She cocks an eyebrow and waves a finger at me. "And you, Minion One, behave. Or I'm revoking your Minion status."

The two girls giggle. Bart presses his fists into his waist. The beautiful Ms. Frasier watches me with just enough mock in her sternness to make wonderful memories for all the kids.

And just enough of a grin to make a wonderful memory for me.

I TIE THE PINK T-SHIRT AROUND MY HEAD, LAWRENCE OF ARABIA style. It's either that or over my shoulders like a cape, and I rather the kids stop with the superhero stuff. As, it seems, would the lovely Ms. Frasier. A couple of the other teachers glare at me because I broke protocol and a rash of t-shirt tying imitation swept the group, but I'd rip the seams of the thing if I put it on.

And no one needs to see me change. The kids don't need to see my scars.

I take my little group out into the field, Bart in front, the girls in the middle, and me following behind. They each carry a plastic basket to collect their berries, but I suspect more will go straight into mouths than into the containers. They're so excited they all but run into the rows of low bushy plants. They fall into parallel picking, very much like they would fall into parallel play, the way the many parenting books I read while recovering said they would.

The field smells like Bart's favorite juice boxes, but real. Dots of bright red berries peek out from under all the deep green leaves. My feet sink into the dirt, but not too far. Walking behind the kids is comfortable, considering.

The pretty Ms. Frasier herds her group in front of ours and when she bends over to help a student, I get a spectacular view of her perfect, round backside. No flab there, just one smoothly curved ass. Great for grabbing onto.

Bart tugs on my shorts. "Are you going back to work after, Daddy?" He filled his basket already and is looking up at me with his most plaintive face.

My settlement money went into the house and a good nest egg for Bart's college, and it means I have savings, so I can't go on disability. So I work. Last year, I went out on my own doing inspections and fire system design consulting. I'm doing well, but businesses take time to grow. Today, I'm working with a new builder. A company that, if I'm lucky, might lead to a major contract in a few months. "Sorry, little man. I have a meeting this afternoon."

Bart frowns. "Oh." He holds up his berries. "Will Uncle Tommy be home?"

My brother used to live with us, to help out, but he moved out over the weekend. Bart's bummed. So am I, to be honest. And I no longer have help at home.

Maybe I should ask Ms. Cunningham if she knows anyone. Bart's too important to leave with any old babysitter.

"Uncle Tommy moved to his own place, remember?" I take Bart's hand. "I'll be back when all your classes are done, just like yesterday. Remember that, too?"

"I remember." He points at the main building. "Can we go now?"

The girls are getting tired, as well. Adrenaline wears off fast when you're four. "Depends on what Ms. Frasier says, right?" I call.

She rubs her hands on her pink t-shirt and it pulls tight over her not-too-big and not-too-small breasts.

The woman is freakin' hot. Lusciously lickable and smokin' hot. Curved perfectly to hold up against a wall, level of hot.

Parts of my body I thought I'd locked down and put into storage want out. For a second, I remember how good a woman's fingers feel when they dig into my shoulders, when she's close to coming and she can't stop herself. How incredible her breath will feel on my neck. How intoxicating it is to hear her whisper my name.

I blink and look away from the luscious Ms. Frasier's incredibly hot body. I need to remember who my priority is. And it ain't my cock.

"We tired?" Ms. Frasier asks.

I look over again, determined to be a good dad. I mock yawn and slump my shoulders. "I need a nap."

The girls giggle. Bart, though, rolls his four-year-old eyes. "Daddy! Act like a grown-up!"

Ms. Frasier laughs, and for a moment that hard teacher-parent line evaporates. She's a woman and I'm a man, and we're sharing this moment with the kids. And damn it, it makes her even more beautiful.

"Okay, everyone, line up!" She glances around, doing the teacher counting thing where she instantly knows the exact location of every child. It's impressive.

Smiling again, she shoos me toward the buses. When her group runs by me, she yells, and they slow, falling in line with Bart, Emma, and Mandy. Three paces ahead, they pair off and hold hands, each with their baskets firmly grasped in their other fists.

Ms. Frasier falls in line with me and before I realize it, I'm reaching for her hand, to mimic the kids.

But when my fingers graze her wrist, she looks up, her eyes wide with surprise.

"Sorry!" I jam my hands into my pockets. What am I doing?

She grins and tucks a stray strand of her jet black hair behind her ear. "The pink hat suits you."

We both laugh. The tension eases and I grin, too. "What's your name? If I'm going to accidently hold your hand, I should at least know your first name."

In front of us, the kids take up their places by the school buses. Ms. Cunningham counts them off and sends them in by color groups.

"Camille," my comrade in neon says.

"Camille," I say. A beautiful name for a beautiful woman. "It's nice to meet you."

CHAPTER 3

Camille

One month after the strawberry picking field trip, Bart's taken to spending as much of his days in my room drawing and painting as he's allowed. Getting him to do any other activity takes effort—he's not all that interested in reading or numbers or playing ball. Just colors and lines. But we work at it, and I'm getting him to hold his attention on a few books.

Dan often stays later than the other parents when he comes to pick up Bart. We talk about Bart and his talent, and how the art gene jumped from his father, right over Dan, to Bart. And, it seems, to Dan's brother, Tom.

Two months after the field trip, autumn cools the weather. Bart's now in long sleeves every day, like his dad.

Dan still stays longer, standing in the middle of my room, often close enough we brush elbows, Bart on his hip, smiling his most wonderful smile. He asks questions about my career goals and hopes for the future. He's always attentive, always focused on our conversation, watching me with his mesmerizing eyes. But mostly we talk about the movies we like and the ones we think might be fun for Bart to watch.

By the fourth month, I've learned a lot about running a small business specializing in fire disaster prevention. By the fifth, I also know all about Uncle Tommy's new fiancé and the coming gallery show of his drawings and paintings. About how Uncle Robby is in grad school in a different state and how Bart misses him.

The holidays come. We make special ornament keepsakes, little plastic globes filled with memories from the year. Bart proudly gives his to his father, and Dan, smiling, hands me a lovely apple tied with a gorgeous, intricate bow. "For Bart's best teacher," he says, holding it out. When I take it from his hand, his fingers sweep over mine and that same tingle I felt the first time I saw him jolts through my body like static electricity.

And it becomes oh so very difficult to be professional around Dan Quidell.

By the sixth month after the field trip, I know all about Bart's upcoming fifth birthday party. Uncle Rob will be home this coming weekend to help celebrate. The Quidells are having a family celebration.

Turns out Dan's brother Tom used to live with them, to help with Bart. But he moved out about the time I started at the Community Center daycare and now Dan's handling everything himself.

I can tell. Each day he looks more exhausted than the day before.

And he's been late to pick up Bart a couple of times, when he's driving from the south side of The Cities and hits bad traffic.

Like today.

Dan staggers in, his white button-down shirt wrinkled and his chin covered with what looks like an uncomfortably itchy five o'clock shadow. Bart's resting on a mat, bored, hungry, and half asleep, his backpack next to him.

"I'm sorry." Dan looks around. Bart's the last one out. Again. Dan takes the new artwork from me when I hold it out and looks at it, and his face crinkles up like he's in pain. Which he might be. I know the changing weather makes aches worse.

I asked my mom, a physical therapist, about it. She went on for almost an hour about scars and pulling and old injuries. Now I know every time Dan hitches his hip it must be because his leg hurts. All I want to do is sit him down and rub the muscle until it loosens.

Then straddle his lap, rubbing other, just as hard parts.

I glance away. We both behave professionally because professional is the way we need to behave. Bart's growth and happiness is both our goals.

Even though I think, sometimes, while we stand between the kids' easels, Dan wants to touch me as much as I want to touch him.

But business is business.

Dan looks at Bart's latest puppy picture like he can't decide if he should make a joke about it, feel proud of his son's talent, or just set it down and curl up on the mat with his boy.

"New contract. It's a forty-five minute drive on a good day." He glances at the window. "Traffic's terrible."

"Could your brother pick him up on days you're late?" Dan needs relief. Running your own business is hard enough, but to do it as a single parent, as well? I don't know how he's still conscious by the end of the week. His weekend evenings are probably consumed by account work and balancing checkbooks, as it is.

Fear flashes through Dan's eyes. Fear like he'd just opened a cabin door to find the movie monster shambling toward him. Like his zombies just caught up.

"No, no, no we're not kicking out Bart. Don't worry." I touch his elbow and my fingers glide over the cotton of his shirt. I know I shouldn't. But my hand reaches anyway, fingers meaning to give reassurance.

Dan nods and I realize I've never seen him in short sleeves. Not even when it was blisteringly hot outside. His shirt feels rough, like no one ever taught him how to care for laundry and keep his clothes soft.

He glances at the mat.

Bart sits up and stretches. "I'm hungry."

Dan's eyes close and I swear he's counting. His shoulders roll back, and when he opens his eyes again, he smiles and holds his arms out to his son. "Come here, little man."

Bart runs to his father and Dan hoists him up. Bart's thumb moves into his mouth and he sucks on it for two quick pulls, then seems to realize what he's doing. His hand vanishes around his daddy's neck.

I want to take Bart and give him a hug. Damn it, I want to give *Dan* a hug. I want to stroke his hair and whisper to him that it's okay. He can rest.

"Are you still looking for help? Sandy said a while ago you were looking for a babysitter. I'm available." The words roll out of my mouth on their own. But damn it, Dan needs help. And honestly, I still need that second job. I nod toward Bart, doing my best to be professional. "I can bring him home on the nights you're running late. *We'll* make dinner. Right?"

Bart nods, but he's too tired and his thumb makes its way into his mouth again.

I can't read what's flitting over Dan's face. Concern? Relief? Disbelief? He looks shocked. He hugs Bart to his shoulder. "My schedule isn't always set."

"That's fine." I tap Bart's arm. "Would that be okay with you? We could paint some more."

He smiles as he nods.

"I'll pay what you need."

I look up at Dan Quidell's handsome face and all I see is hope. And thankfulness. He's looking at me like a man chased by monsters who believes he's about to get eaten. He can't believe I just offered an escape. "As long as I have enough to pay my rent and my school loans and still eat, I'm good."

The disbelief turns into a big smile and he turns to his son. "I gotta put you down for a second, buddy. Okay?"

Bart nods and Dan sets him on his feet before digging in his back pocket for his wallet. "Do you have a pen?"

I grab one off my desk.

"Thanks." Dan pulls out a business card and flips it over. "Address. My cell number's on the front. Can you come by tonight? After work?"

I take the card. They live three miles away. "I'll be by in an hour."

Dan, smiling, hoists up Bart again. "Should we make Ms. Frasier dinner, little man?"

Bart blinks. "Mac and cheese?"

I laugh. "I like mac and cheese, too!"

"Dinner it is." Dan extends his hand to shake.

His palm feels strong and warm, his skin wonderfully male, and the tingle moves from my fingers up my arm. Six months of talking every day, of sharing about Bart, of me silently and unprofessionally lusting for this fantastic man, and this will be the first time we see each other outside of work.

"Thank you." Dan grips Bart, smiling again.

"You're welcome," I say, as I watch Dan carry his son through the whooshing door. They're gone, into the evening's setting sun, but I still feel Dan's hand on mine.

CHAPTER 4

Daniel

I hand a plate to Bart. "Set it on the table, buddy."

He nods and walks slowly out of our open kitchen toward the dining area. Next to the table, just outside the patio door, snow covers the deck I added as part of my therapy. Doc told me to keep moving, so I kept moving. There's something meditative about swinging a hammer.

I almost sold the house and all the memories of my ex when I received the settlement, but I didn't want to give her that satisfaction. So I remodeled instead. It's an open floor plan, with stairs to the second floor next to the front door and a walkout basement tucked underneath. This floor is mostly kitchen and living room.

Now it's ours, Bart and me. I built him a nice home. And my ex-wife is somewhere, presumably living in the woods in one of the big square states out west with her newest boyfriend. The farther she is from sane people, the better the world will function.

Bart grips the plate as he shuffles along the hardwood into the dining area and to Camille. She watches, letting him set the table one plate and spoon at a time, and smiles every time he looks over the table's edge at his work. He's doing his "arranging" thing again, making the plates and the silverware into pictures.

When he makes a smiley face with his plate, a spoon, and two strawberries from the fridge, she claps and gives him a hug.

And all I can do is hope I can pay her well enough to make watching Bart worth her time.

I carry the dish of mac and cheese to the table. I made spinach salads too, with some other strawberries, and a vinaigrette. Bart thought I was crazy for putting berries on *spinach*.

Camille watches me as I sit down. My leg hurts more than usual today. My shoulder, as well. I should probably put heat on them after she leaves, though I wonder how her fingers massaging the tightness away would feel. Rubbing across my shoulders, her breasts pressed against my back.

I force the thoughts away. This is not a business relationship I'm going to mess up no matter how beautiful she is. Bart's too important.

Camille eats her mac and cheese, commenting on how good it is, and says she likes the salad. Bart, proud, launches into a detailed description of how he took out the vinegar and the shaker and helped measure *and* pour, though he still refuses to try the salad, instead sticking to dipping his strawberries into his whipped topping.

After dinner, Camille helps me get him into bed, even reading him his bedtime story. We both tuck him in and he cuddles in safe wearing his superhero jammies holding his superhero beanie toys.

I close down his door.

"I'll help clean up." Camille points down the stairs before jamming her hands into her pockets.

She'll stay a little longer. I grin and follow her down to the kitchen, letting myself watch her walk, knowing she can't see me appreciating the luscious curve of her lower back.

She's average height, the top of her head coming in under my chin, and she's smoothly round. Her teacher-clothes hide her shape, but it's still obvious. And it's nice.

At least I'll get to look at a pretty woman when I come home from work, even if touching will be out of the question.

"Do you work out?" After six months of chatting every day, I know a lot about her life, except her exercise habits. The question, though, slips out of my mouth before I realize I have no right to ask. And that it makes it obvious I've been looking at her ass.

So I try to climb out of the hole I just dug. "I mean, if helping out interferes with your routine. I have equipment here. It's downstairs. I got it because my doctors and therapists said I should and when Bart was a baby I couldn't go to a gym. I'd put him in his playpen and he'd watch. Usually demanding I take him out. You're welcome to use it."

From over her shoulder, I see Camille grinning. She's probably wondering why I keep talking. *I* don't know why I keep talking.

At the bottom of the stairs, she's still grinning. "My apartment complex has this crappy little workout room and there's usually some creepy guy in there." She rolls her eyes. "The Community Center is too expensive. So yeah, that'd be nice."

Her eyes are the richest, most vibrant dark brown I have ever seen. They're like melted chocolate. I nod and look away, absently rubbing at my neck. I drop my hand when I realize what I'm doing.

Camille frowns. "Is it bad tonight?"

"What?" Is she asking about my workout equipment? I must be making a weird face because she chuckles.

"I can tell when you hurt. It shows in how you move." She points at my shoulder. "I used to dance. When I was in school." Shrugging, she walks into the living room. "It's obvious."

She's a dancer? No wonder she moves with such grace. And has such a nice ass.

"Sit down." A hint of commanding teacher rolls out in her voice when she points at the chair.

What am I supposed to do? She's Ms. Frasier and I have to do what she says. I drop into the chair with the low back Tom placed next to the couch. My brother stood in my living room when he moved in, staring at my hand-me-down furniture, and said if I'm going to live with Dad's cast-offs, I should at least not arrange them exactly the way he had.

I hadn't realized.

Now, Camille moves behind the chair I'm dutifully sitting in, and dances her fingers over my shoulder muscles.

Her touch is firm through my shirt and a little cool, as if her hands are cold. I want to grasp them between my own. Give her my warmth.

"You have an asymmetry here, in your neck muscles." Her fingers press and for the briefest moment, her breasts brush against the back of my head. "Let's try this."

I want to pull her over my shoulder and onto my lap. I want her to smooth those dexterous fingers over my chest before she wraps her arms around my head and rubs her hands over my neck and my back. I want to feel her fingers in my hair. On my scalp. To breathe in her scent, a warm mixture of brightly-colored art supplies and sweet woman. Sweet, like she uses a natural shampoo and soap, ones with a fruit scent.

If I lick between her breasts, will I taste it?

Her fingers skip up the sides of my neck, then down again, before thumbs press into my flesh.

In just the right spot. With just the right pressure.

My thoughts flip from wanting her touch to feeling all its brilliance. My entire neck releases and a wave of relief flows down my spine. Rolls down and through my hips until it pools in my groin. Her breasts brush against my head again and I hear her feet reposition on the carpet. She's going to press into my neck again.

"You're an angel." She is. One perfect and wonderful angel. Six months quietly trying to learn everything I could about her life and I never, not once, caught a hint of this particular skill.

Now I'm wondering what else I don't know.

I *want* to know.

Camille chuckles and presses again, this time on my deltoids. "My mom is a physical therapist. I was considering going into it, but I like to teach. Watching the kids paint and draw is its own magic." She presses again. "I do wish there were more art therapy jobs."

More tension releases and that feeling I had when I first saw her, when I went on the field trip with Bart's class, follows the leaving aches. The joy that comes with seeing beauty, that moment of understanding I'm in the presence of someone special, flows into my body. It's warm and crackling, like a campfire. It pushes out all the pains and I sigh.

Me, Daniel Quidell, ex-firefighter, lets out a less-than-manly sigh of relief.

Her hands fold over my shoulders and it's not just her fingers on my body anymore. Her palms lay flat against my shirt.

I want to pull off the collar around my neck. Tear off the fabric over my shoulders. To have her skin against mine—*all* of her skin— would prove once and for all that she is the angel I think she is.

But my scars might scare her away and she's the best thing that could possibly have happened to Bart.

"How much does it hurt?" The teacher tones of her voice have fallen away and she's replaced them with sympathy. Or maybe, I wonder, if what I'm hearing is empathy. She's almost whispering.

Could I be so lucky to hear empathy? "I'm conscious of it most of the time." There's really no other way to describe it. The aches and the pains don't leave. They're always there.

"They're background." I shrug. "You know how when it's cold outside and your joints seem to slow down and you can't ignore it completely? Like what should flow smoothly is clogged up by slush and you have to wait longer than you expect to get through? It's like that. When my shoulder pings, I know it's there."

One of her hands lifts off my shoulder and she moves around to the front of the chair. The other hand slides along my skin and my shirt bunches up under her fingers.

For a second, she looks at her fingers and not my face. "The massage helps?"

More than she knows. More than I can verbalize. Her touch, even through the fabric, is warm and soothing and better than any of my therapists'.

She must have read my relief from my body because a smile lights up her beautiful face. She's got a golden tone to her and the loveliest skin I have ever seen.

"Before I go, we're going to make sure you sleep well tonight." Her hand lifts off my shoulder as she nods toward the kitchen. "Do you have avocado oil?"

"Avocados have oil?" We eat healthy but Bart hates avocados so I stick with olive oil.

Camille grins and shakes her head. "It'll help with the massage."

"Oh." That means she wants me to take off my shirt. *Maybe I can get her to take off hers*, I think. Then I realize what that means. If this gets weird, she might not want to help anymore, and I can't do that to Bart.

And she'll see my scars.

Her head tips to the side. "You look conflicted."

The light filtering in from the kitchen halos around her head until she drops onto the couch.

I swear she's carried the light with her. That it's still there, in her hair, and on her fingers. Camille's surrounded by angelfire.

God damn, she's beautiful.

"I'm sorry," she whispers, her face suddenly as pained as my back felt. "I just thought that maybe I could help you as well. Not just Bart." She pats her thigh and smiles. "Tell you what. Let's make arrangements for Monday. You said you have another late meeting, right?"

All I want is to kiss her. To lay her down on the couch and press kisses over every inch of her skin. The lovely sweep of her neck. The exceptional roundness of her breasts. I want to take the wonder of her touch and give it right back to her as gentle rubs and hard thrusts.

I don't dare stand up. I feel my heart beating and my cock is pulsing right along with it.

"Late meeting," I say. Only those two words will leave my mouth. If I don't shut it right now, my lips are going to be nibbling on her earlobe.

"Do you want me to bring Bart home? We'll make dinner." She smiles again and I swear the halo has returned. The squiggles covering her loose-fitting blouse draw my attention but I can't stare at her chest. I know those buttons will pop right off the fabric if I rip it from her body. Pop like little corn kernels and bounce across the living room.

Nodding, she stands. "I have the key you gave me before dinner and the extra booster seat in my car. Bart and I have the routine down."

She rubs her hands over her belly the way she did on the field trip and I almost scoop her up. I'd make it up the stairs and into the bedroom before I got winded. I can still pass all the state firefighter requirements.

Except for the metal in my bones and the scars on my skin.

"If you want me to do your pressure points again, just ask." Camille tips her head again and her face is intense, the way I imagine she watches a student who is upset. She's gauging what she needs to do to calm me down.

And I don't know what to do. Bart needs her. So I better not mess this up.

I stand slowly and slide my fists into my pockets to disguise my rock hard cock as best I can. "Next week, then."

She glances at my crotch and I swear her eyebrows arch in approval.

If only I could be so lucky. But she hasn't actually seen my shoulder yet.

Camille nods before picking up her purse. At the door, she smiles again, and I lean against the frame.

"Good night, Dan." With that, she walks to her little compact car waiting at the end of my driveway.

I close the door. The house suddenly feels worn. My furniture isn't mine. It's no one's, to be honest. Except the kid's art table and easel, in the corner. And the two boxes full of action figures. And the stacks of cartoon DVDs.

But when Bart's asleep, there's not a lot here.

I stand straight. This is the world I've built, and I should be proud of it. My son has a bright future.

I'll count in and count out, forcing my libido to calm the fuck down. I'll stand in the damned shower and take care of it myself. Though this time, I suspect my mind is going to wander to a real woman.

But I won't let it. I can't interfere with what I mean to provide my son. Because everything's for Bart.

CHAPTER 5

Camille

W hy the hell did I just stand up and leave like that? And now I'm driving home. Down the dark suburban streets toward my apartment building. Alone.

Again, that most unteacher-like word reverberates through my head: *Fuck*.

The raw need on Dan's face alone almost brought on an orgasm. When has a man ever reacted to me like that? I touched his shoulders and he was instantly hard. Hard enough his erection clearly wanted release.

His *huge* erection.

Maybe I imagined the whole damned thing. But I couldn't let his neck hurt him like that. But I wasn't expecting that response. He's a parent. A *gorgeous* parent.

I slap the steering wheel of my pathetic little hatchback. Damn it, I just wanted to help.

My head's spinning. I park in my building's lot and stare at the crummy entrance of my low rent apartment. Babysitting will help me make ends meet. I have to remember that.

And, I think, that's why Dan didn't touch. Business is business. He sees me as someone trustworthy with his boy.

I close my eyes, fighting my body's need to cry. I feel a tear anyway. Why am I reacting this way?

But I know. A man with a heart as good as Dan's deserves the most respect and the best treatment I have to offer.

And he's going to get it.

WHEN DAN DROPS OFF BART MONDAY MORNING, WE CHAT SOME. He stands an extra foot or so away, as if he's afraid I'll jump into his arms. Or that, maybe, he'll throw me down on top of my desk, both our jobs be damned. I can't tell. But his gaze makes my skin heat. It's hard not to fan myself like some belle.

He tells me he needs to grocery shop, but there's leftover mac and cheese, and fruit on the counter. And that he will be home about nine or nine-thirty.

I watch him dodge incoming kids and exercise class participants as he strides toward the Community Center exit. He spends more time watching me than where he's walking.

Bart spends the day extra chatty and happy as he moves back and forth between Sandy's room and mine. By the end of the day, all the kids know that I'm his new babysitter. I field question after question about why Bart gets a teacher babysitter and the other kids don't.

A couple of the teachers seem annoyed.

It's not against the rules to babysit outside of work hours. I think they're more upset about who I'm sitting for, not that I'm doing the work.

Dan seems oblivious. Not once in the past six months have I seen his eyes roam over any of the other teachers or moms, or any of the women in their tight workout clothes who take the fitness classes on the other side of the Community Center. He's focused on Bart. And chatting with me.

At ten after five, the last of my other kids leaves with his mom, and it's just Bart and me. He bounces over, his big blue eyes wide, and takes my hand. "I ride in your car tonight! Daddy's truck is *big*."

A lot about Dan Quidell is big. But I can't think about the hard lines of his big body right now. I have a room to tidy.

I kneel down so I'm eye-to-eye with Bart. "We need to clean up first. Will you help me?"

Bart's little arms wrap around my neck and I'm suddenly gripped tightly by a wonderful Quidell man. "You're pretty," he says.

I pick him up, hugging him just as tightly as he's hugging me. "And you are quite a handsome young man."

When I put him down, he helps me clean up by putting all the papers into the recycling. And when we leave, he holds tight to my hand, his superhero backpack over his arms, and together, we go home.

❦

BART'S DETERMINED TO STAY AWAKE FOR HIS DAD. HE CUDDLES against my side on the couch in his superhero pajamas, one of his superhero action figures in his hand, and we settle in to watch super- hero cartoons. Garishness pops and giggles from the television but he's asleep within fifteen minutes.

His little head smells like kid's shampoo. He'd been so good all evening, doing his chores and following me around the house, to make sure I knew where all the dishes went, where the towels were, and what temperature his bath was supposed to be. He lined up all his superheroes on the lip of the tub, talking to each in turn, and washed his hair all by himself.

The beautiful child leaning against me trusts me enough to fall asleep on my arm. I hoist him up carefully and he mumbles a word.

A word that sounds faintly like "Mommy."

But he couldn't have said "Mommy." He doesn't see her. Hell, from the file, I doubt he even knows what she looks like.

Bart wraps his legs around my waist and I carry him upstairs. He's getting big, but I manage. In his room, I tuck him in and set his nightlight.

The door creaks as I close it, and suddenly I'm alone in the Quidell house. Downstairs, the refrigerator clunks to life. The television is on mute, but light reflecting up the steps jumps and jitters with the still-playing cartoon characters. Their house smells clean but also like men live here. There's no subtle hint of flowers, or sweetness.

I breathe in. Sandalwood.

The door to Dan's bedroom is half closed and I stare from my spot in front of Bart's. I see the outline of a messy bed, but no overt signs of clutter. Or clothes on the floor.

I turn away, to go downstairs. It's not my business.

Besides, Dan should be home soon.

My foot hits the landing at the bottom of the stairs just as I hear the garage door open. Dan's headlights arch across the front window as he pulls into the driveway, and for a second they overtake the flashing from the cartoon on the television. I click it off and walk toward the kitchen, and the entrance from the garage.

The lock tumbler clicks over and the door opens. Dan swings into the kitchen, glancing around, as if looking for Bart.

"He's asleep," I say, as I come around the corner.

His keys drop onto the counter next to the paper sack he sets down. He blinks his beautiful blue-green eyes, smiling his most wonderful smile, and the next thing I know, he twirls me around in the center of the kitchen. "I got the new account."

"New account?" He didn't say anything about tonight's meeting being a big deal. Only that he'd be late.

"I didn't say anything because I didn't want to jinx it. But I think you're my good luck charm and from now on I'll always tell you. Promise." For a second, he looks like he wants to kiss me.

Then again, he usually looks like he wants to kiss me. Unless I'm imagining that, too.

"Spill it, big guy." I've known Dan Quidell for six months and this is the first time I've seen him not-Bart-associated happy. Real, adult man happy, not just parent happy.

I swear he's standing his full six three-and-a-half height, with his shoulders more square and strong than I've seen before. It suits him.

I like it.

That wonderful swashbuckling smirk of his reappears and I almost sigh. I *am* like some freshman with a crush on the senior quarterback. But this is business, and we're friends, and I won't ruin it—or the evening—for Dan.

He drops his jacket on a chair in the breakfast nook and strides back to the sack on the counter, still smiling. "I got a chardonnay, a pinot noir, and a malbec. Don't know what you like." He holds out all three bottles, two in one hand and the third gripped in the other.

The wines look expensive. "I've never had malbec."

Dan glances at the back of the bottle. "Well, it says here that we will celebrate my new contract with the 'rich splendor of a smooth-but-intense, full of hints of blackberry, Argentinian grape.'"

He winks once before setting down the bottles. "You hungry? I bought cheese." He pulls out a block of equally expensive-looking cheese. "And bread." An artisan loaf follows.

It's like a picnic on the Seine, but with South American wine instead of a French Bordeaux.

"And chocolate." He's grinning like Bart now, as he lifts half a pound of chocolate perfection from the bag. The candy in his hand probably cost as much as the wine.

And he wants to share it with me. "Don't keep secrets, Dan." I'm smiling as much as he is. "Tell me!"

He pulls a couple of glasses out of a cupboard and a nice wooden cutting board from a lower cabinet. After a moment of digging, he pulls a corkscrew from a drawer. "Haven't used this in a while."

I set the cheese on the board. It's soft under its wax coating. There's French on the label. He really did go all out. "Are you going to tell me or not?" I set the bread next to it.

The cork pops from the bottle. Holding the glasses and chocolate in one of his big hands and the bottle in the other, he walks backward toward the living room, still grinning.

I drop onto the couch next to him and set the board on the coffee table. It's an old thing and kind of rickety. I get the impression he doesn't care all that much about the furnishings. Making sure Bart is comfortable seems to take priority.

Dan pours the wine. "It's with a major hotel chain. They're

upgrading seven of their buildings here in The Cities and the firm brought me on for the duration of the contract."

"That's wonderful!" He's been in business on his own for a year and he's already making good.

"There's more." He takes a sip before slicing us each some cheese and bread.

I take a sip. The wine is smooth and rich, like he described, and has a wonderful layered depth missing from the cheap stuff. "This is good."

"Try this." He holds out a piece of cheese he's set on a small bit of bread.

I lean forward and wrap my lips around the food, taking it from his fingers with my teeth.

Dan's face changes. The little boy exuberance suddenly contracts. His focus is completely on me.

It feels wonderful. He watches my mouth and raw need winks through his features again, the way it did last night.

I want to push him against the couch cushions and lay kisses across the stubble coating his jaw. To run my hands over the biceps straining the fabric of his wrinkled button-down. I want so very much to feel him thrusting into me with what I whole-heartedly suspect is a cock worthy of his big, gorgeous body.

I look away. I can't think of him that way. He is, technically, my boss, even if he's the hottest boss on the planet and a man who wants to celebrate his accomplishments with me.

"Turns out the firm doing the remodel has offices in seven other states. If they do well here, there's a good chance the contract will go national, and me with it."

"That's great!" Not hugging him takes considerable effort. I take another sip of my wine.

His smile fades as he slices us more cheese. It's as smooth as the wine, and perfect with the bread. Perfect, like Mr. Dan Quidell.

"It'll mean more time away from Bart. More late nights. And travel." He taps the edge of the cutting board, and doesn't look up.

He can't think like that. He's an excellent father.

I touch his arm, so he'll look at me. "Do you want the extended contract?"

Dan's eyes widen. He nods and his smile returns. "Yes."

"Then you work for it. Bart will be fine. He's a bright kid. Besides, it won't be long before he's in kindergarten. It'll get easier. I promise."

Dan breathes in and out and his shoulders straighten as if I just lifted off the weight of the world. "You're right." Sipping his wine, he sits back. "I worry too much."

"Yes, you do." I sit back as well. The cheese isn't slowing down the alcohol from hitting my bloodstream and a buzz starts. "I better wait before driving home." I wave my hand at my glass. "I don't drink often and I'm a lightweight."

"A lightweight with a beautiful soul." Dan laughs and hands me another piece of cheese. "With beautiful eyes to match."

I don't know what to say. He's watching me the way he was earlier. If he puts the same focus on his work, he'll be unstoppable. No wonder they chose him for the contract.

"I inherited them from my Maori grandmother."

His surprise quickly turns to admiration and he raises his glass to me. "A Norse king, at least one Highlander family, and a rumored Brazilian professional wrestler. Don't know for sure." The swashbuckling grin returns.

I laugh. "No wonder you're big and broad."

"And no wonder you're lovely." His gaze feels like he's physically touching me. I want to moan.

It's almost too much and I look away. "I had an ex tell me I look like a demon because they're so dark." I roll my eyes.

"Jerk *and* an idiot." Dan frowns again, but this time, the focus remains. If my ex was here, I suspect Dan would have punched him.

"Oh." My lips round and I think I'm blinking. Dan is wonderful. And handsome. And intense. And...

Maybe it's the wine. Or maybe he makes me a little drunk. But I lean in and kiss his cheek.

CHAPTER 6

Camille

The raw need returns to Dan's face, but this time I feel it vibrate from the strong fingers he curls around my elbows. He won't let me pull away.

His kiss bends me back. He pulls my bottom lip between his, then my top, as if he's tasting me the way he tasted the wine. My body stops everything—breathing, thinking, moving—so it can concentrate on the feel of his mouth and the touch of his fingers.

One hand moves up and cups my shoulder, pulling me closer. The other moves to the side of my rib cage, next to my breast. He doesn't grope or cop a feel, but his thumb is right there, ready, perfectly positioned to sweep over my nipple.

He pulls back just enough for me to inhale, then his mouth is on mine again, working across my lips from one corner to the other. He tastes like the wine and a little like the cheese, but mostly I sense *Dan*, his strength and his masculine hardness. And I want more.

A lot more. Every muscle of his body moving against mine. Every kiss.

His forehead touches my cheek before he pulls back. "I'm sorry. I
—" His face crinkles up. "It's been a while since—" His mouth closes
into a thin line.

"You're worrying too much again."

The next kiss drops me onto the cushions. Dan's lips work along
my jaw, down my neck, and back up to my earlobe. His breath fills my
ear, warm and strong, like him.

I wiggle, curling my legs around his waist, and pull him close
enough his erection rubs against my belly.

A quiet moan rolls from his chest and he pushes up, off my body.
On one arm. He's planking on the couch, over me, using one arm, and
looking at my face as if he's completely unconscious of his body's
effort.

"*Ohhhh...* you are so strong." I run my hands over his chest,
wiggling again. I won't run this time. I know he worries and I know I
should too, but I have to have him. Even if it's only once. "I'm on the
pill and I had all the tests after that jerk told me I had demon eyes."

Dan runs his free hand over my breasts, staring like he's never
touched nipples before. Staring with utter joy and exuberance. For me.

I yank his shirt out and push my hands up under the fabric, feeling
the ripples of his abs. I have to see. I *need* to see. "Take off your shirt."

He sits up before I finish the sentence, but he's not pulling off his
shirt. He sits back.

"What's wrong?" Did I move too fast? Does his shoulder hurt from
holding himself up? I reach for him but he catches my hand.

Dan closes his eyes as he pulls my fingers to his lips. Slowly, gently,
he kisses my knuckles, his lips reverent as they explore my skin, and
my body aches for him. But I see the tension in his shoulders again.

"Do you hurt? Do you—"

His next kiss silences my questions. I melt against his chest, all my
thoughts folded up and set aside by his embrace. But he pulls
back again.

He looks down as he unbuttons the first button of his shirt. The
second button releases and I fumble with the one at the bottom,
working up as he works down. His chest over his heart appears first

and I see a gentle sweep of hair. Under my fingers, his abs tighten and release as he works his shirt. His skin and his muscles are shadowed, but I see the definition.

He truly is gorgeous.

With the last one, I tug at the fabric, my need to feel his skin too much. I want him *now*. I want to be on top so I can rub his abs and kiss his chest. I want to feel his large hands cup my breasts as I ride his cock.

I want, more than anything, to be with Dan not as his son's babysitter. Not as a teacher. As a woman.

He holds my wrists again. Softly, but he doesn't want me to push back his shirt. "I have scars, Camille. From the fire and the operations."

My brow crinkles and I bite my lip. How bad can they be? He has use of his shoulder and leg, even if it's diminished. "Dan, I don't care. Unless you're all furry like a werewolf. And bark. I don't like guys who bark."

He chuckles and quickly kisses me on the lips. The shirt slips off his shoulders.

I see what he's been hiding. And I see why I've never seen him in a short sleeved shirt.

The skin across his shoulder looks pock-marked, as if someone punched hole after hole into his deltoid. A big v-shaped surgical scar caps his shoulder and pulls the marks like someone had played connect-the-dot. Down his arm, the scar takes on a more hamburger-like texture just above his elbow. Along either side of the joint are two more long surgical scars.

The scars from what must have been skin grafts extend onto his chest and probably onto his back. He turns slightly, showing me his side. The grafts halt as he moves, not stretching. Dan has an inflexible quilt from his collarbone to his shoulder, down the side of his chest, and a narrow band running down his hip. The patch vanishes under his waistband and I suspect it doesn't end until it reaches his knee.

"Three pins here." He points to his shoulder and his elbow. "And two here." His finger moved to his thigh. "My friend Jason hauled me out. He ended up with pretty bad nerve damage. Ended his career, too."

The scars feel bumpy and areas don't feel quite alive. Like they're rubber. But they're not. They may block part of his life, but they're part of the man in front of me.

"Dan." I pull him to me, kissing his neck and his chin.

He responds immediately, yanking my shirt up and over my head. A deep, throaty growl rolls from him the moment he sees my black lacy bra. I don't have nice clothes, but sometimes I buy sexy underwear.

I put some on this morning, hoping. Dan does not disappoint.

He buries his face in my cleavage and makes little yipping noises, like he's a werewolf puppy. Laughing, I unhook my bra, freeing my breasts.

The other men I've been with always seemed to ignore my chest. I'm not huge, but I'm not small, either. They seemed to look at my boobs, nod, and get on to the business that interested them the most.

Not Dan. He palms my breasts and sucks a nipple into his mouth, humming the entire time. The vibration feels wonderful and I release a growl just as throaty as his.

"You are heavenly." I barely hear him. He scoots down and nips at the skin on the underside of my breasts.

I'm panting. He has me *panting* and we're still half dressed.

Maybe he'll be the one. I don't orgasm easily. Never have, no matter how much I want a guy. But Dan's incredible. The electricity is back and it's sparking across my skin every time he sweeps his fingers over my belly or his lips over my nipples.

I pull on his shoulders. "Kiss me."

The look on Dan's face is, I think, the happiest I've ever seen a man during sex. He immediately covers my mouth with his, but he's careful. Slow. And his big, strong arms curl under my back, lifting me off the couch.

He wants this to last. He *wants* to kiss me, like it's important.

"Dan..." I manage to get his name out between our lips. He's holding me off the couch, up toward his body, and I feel like I'm floating. Oh God, Dan makes me float.

It might happen. He might be the one to do it.

"I've wanted to kiss you every day for the last six months." His muscles hum under my hands.

Six months and I've wanted much more than to kiss him. I reach for the fly of his pants because I need him *right now*. Every muscle in my body shudders the way my nipples did when he curled his tongue around them. I see only the beautiful man kneeling between my legs. Hear only his steady breathing and the wonderful sound of first the button of his pants releasing, then the zipper.

But he stops and his eyes narrow. A hand cups a breast again. This time, he's not gentle. This time, he pinches. "Take off your pants."

I immediately unzip my jeans and wiggle them down my hips, revealing my matching little black lace panties. Dan growls again and before I have my jeans off my thighs, he grabs the fabric and yanks them down and off my legs. They snap against the wall next to the television, knocking one of his brother's lovely paintings, but Dan doesn't notice. He kneads my hips, his thumbs rubbing over the lace covering my pussy, his face focused and very, very intense.

A thumb sweeps under the fabric. "God damn you are *wet*."

I feel the tingle that happens before an orgasm. The fluttering and the overload like I just put something in my mouth that's more flavorful than my tongue can handle. I suck in my breath and Dan is on me, covering me completely with his big, hard body.

His next kiss takes away all the breath I just pulled in. He takes it and gives it back, his fingers curling into my hair, his hand gripping the side of my head. "My angel," he whispers.

I can't speak. Words don't form. My panties snap across the room, following my jeans, and Dan grunts, his shoulders twisting and contorting.

He's pulling off his pants.

Time all but stops. I hear the dull clinking of his zipper against his belt buckle. The fabric of his chinos wisps. The waistband of his boxers snap against his skin and another grunt pops from his throat and against the skin of my neck.

How can it take so long to get off a pair of—

He pushes into me faster and harder than I expect, his face still against my shoulder. I buck against his thrust, overwhelmed by his size. I rake my nails over his shoulders, stuttered whimpers lifting from my throat. His thrust hurts but it doesn't *hurt*. It fills. Dan fills me all the way to my spine.

He stops moving, his big body frozen like he's been encased in a block of ice. Like that slush he talked about Friday night, the cold that makes his joints hurt, suddenly solidified around his entire body.

"Did I hurt you?" His beautiful eyes show more concern than I've ever seen from a lover. He still doesn't move. "It's been—"

I kiss him the way he kissed me—deeply, our lips bruising, our breath mingling.

He moans into my mouth as he thrusts again. Just once. And stops. Again.

He lifts himself up just enough we can see each other clearly.

The men I've been with controlled their facial expressions, and right now I see Dan trying to do the same thing. I see the *I'm cool* and the *Fuck yeah* that guys think they're supposed to show. But I see something else, too. Something intense. And I can't tell if it's joy or need or thankfulness. Or maybe it's all three.

Then it's gone as if he's burying it in snow. It washes out into the *I'm cool* and damn it, I want it back. I don't know why, but I do. Because deep inside, I know it's special.

He moves deeper and I feel the same extra physical intensity I feel when a man blindfolds me during sex. That same extra enhancement of every little sound, every little flavor on a man's lips or the tip of his cock. Every extra wave of electricity through every single nerve-ending brushing the surface of my skin.

Whatever his look meant, whatever the emotion he's feeling that he thinks he needs to cover up, makes *me* feel alive.

"Dan," I whisper. I curl my fingers into the muscles of his strong backside, my nails digging in just a little. Just enough to pull his attention to his own skin. And I move my hands a little up, then a little down, in the rhythm I like.

Because I think he's the one who's going to do it. "I want you to come inside me," I rasp.

His eyes close and his mouth opens. A shiver moves through his entire body. "Holy hell," he groans. His abs lift off me as he curls his body so he can kiss my neck.

He's not pumping. He pushes in gradually, his hips swirling in a just as slow, just as careful corkscrew motion and it's almost too much. I feel the head of his cock pulse with each slide in, and the pull of the suction caused by each slide out.

It's magic.

"What are you doing to me?" I'm panting again. I haven't been with a lot of guys, but enough to get a sense of what they like. And to learn a few tricks to heighten sensation enough so I can come. But most of my ex-boyfriends just liked to fuck.

Dan stops moving again. He's deep enough not to break the internal vacuum he's created, but he's just barely inside me.

The electric feeling he caused with his gaze snaps across my abdomen, this time created by his cock.

"I..." His tongue traces my lips when he kisses me, and his teeth glide over my cheek like he wants to bite, but he doesn't move his cock deeper. "You don't like it?"

A micro-expression flashes over his face so fast I don't know if I truly see it. Maybe I'm picking up something else from his body. But I swear I see *Oh shit I'm doing it wrong*.

"This is the best sex I have ever had," I blurt out. "And you just started. Oh my God." My head tilts back and I moan. "I like it a lot."

His eyes and his mouth round into perfect circles but the new expression vanishes as fast as the one before it.

And I'm drowning in a new kiss.

A deep, wonderful, intense kiss that flows through his neck to his shoulder muscles under my gripping hands. I run my fingers down his spine, feeling the joy I feel on his lips work through his body and loosen all the knots along his backbone.

The dancing emotions resurface across his face. The skin around his eyes tightens and loosens, pulls and releases. His cheeks do the same. He's trying to control his expressions, but he's not good at it.

For a second, I wonder how much practice he's had.

He presses his forehead against my temple. "I want to be with you."

His words come out fast, their tone tightening and loosening like his expression. Like he's been fighting their escape. But they're out now, between us.

"You're with me right now." I kiss the bridge of his nose.

Deep inside my heart, in that same place where I know what his expressions mean, I hear a little voice: *I want it to always be like this.*

The rounding of his eyes and mouth happen again, until it vanishes into his next kiss. Slowly, he moves into me again. I think he's testing to see how deep he can thrust. How much of him I can take. I rock my hips and with each push I stretch a little more. And each time, a new shiver rolls through Dan.

"If I move faster, I'll..." He groans into my ear. "I haven't done this in..." Another groan. "You feel so damned *good.*"

The electricity fires through me again and I think it might happen. He's not actively rubbing my clit. Just pressing his pelvis against it so excruciatingly slowly.

I need more.

"Do it." I want this to last but I want him to pound me. I want his fingers gripping my shoulder and I want to see him on the edge. I want his body hitting mine *just right.*

He stops again, but this time he looks puzzled.

"Please." I pant again. I want every single inch, every single kiss Dan has to offer. I rock my hips against his.

When he whispers my name, my world implodes. I feel the living warmth of his healthy skin, and the cool shell of his scars. I feel him watching me carefully and adjusting how he holds his hips to pull the most moans from my throat. But mostly I feel Dan letting go.

The wonderful man—the brilliant, caring man—pumping into me becomes everything, and I kiss him with all that flows through me.

I weave my fingers into his hair, holding tight as his speed increases. He fucks wonderfully—absolutely, incredibly *wonderfully.* Hard, smooth. Shifting, he rises up and slams against my clitoris.

My moan surprises me. I always need fingers, slaps. A vibrator. But the moan starts in my belly and rips with lightning speed up my spine and out through my open mouth.

I immediately realize how loud I am and I slap my hand over my mouth, quelling the sound.

But I still feel that need. I'm so close. On the edge.

Dan stops thrusting but stays buried in me, and kisses along my fingers, grinning like he won best in show.

"Don't stop." Damn it, I need everything he's got.

His next thrust pushes me up the pillow under my back.

"I don't always orgasm," I whisper.

Dan stops again. "What?"

"Dan! You're *excruciating*!" I dig my nails into his backside.

Another hard thrust slams me into the pillows. "Good excruciating or bad excruciating?" His eyes say his question is serious.

"Good... good... but I need more."

He smirks his pirate smile. "Tell me what you need."

I kiss him and he stops chuckling. His gaze stays locked to mine, his face still intense. Still focused.

"What you're doing. Don't stop." I want to come at the same time as *this* man. No one else. Him.

He rolls his hips in a way I didn't know possible when he thrusts and I want to yelp again. I want to shout and yell and make sure he knows how intense he feels. How deep he's inside me.

I tighten my lower abs and we arch together; clench together. Dan responds with a shudder and another moan, and a deeper, harder thrust.

His back tightens under my palms. His abs curl and his arms quake. He presses his face against my neck, his mouth locked against my skin, and I feel his deep baritone more than hear it. His cock pulses sharply and I feel it through my hips.

"I..." he whispers. "*Oh*..."

I feel his frenzy ebbing away as his lips dance over mine. His body's relaxing.

"Could you..." I wiggle under him. "I need a little..."

Dan grabs my hips as he sits up, keeping my pussy against his pelvis and his cock deep inside me.

The pad of his thumb taps around my opening. He's looking for my clit.

When he finds it, my back arches.

"There?" Each new rub carries more pressure. "Tell me when it's right." He watches my pussy—watches his not-yet soft cock glide slowly in and out with each of twirl of his thumb—like he's looking at the most beautiful work of art in the world.

His look alone is enough. The muscles of my pelvis and my belly contract. And another loud moan rips from my throat.

"*Fuck*." Dan falls on top of me. He manages to keep his thumb between us somehow.

Another wave of the orgasm rocks up my spine.

"That work?" he asks.

"Ummm...." I can't get out an answer. Not as words.

He tries to move off me but I keep him where he is.

I kiss his temple. The shoulders of the beautiful man kissing my neck feel calm under my fingers. The tension that had been under my hands has been replaced by an easy looseness.

I kiss his forehead, holding onto this incredible man.

More happiness shows in Dan's eyes than I've ever seen from a man after sex. More calm. And, I think, joy. His kisses show it too, as his lips travel over my chin and jaw, down the side of my neck, onto my shoulder. He's so gentle.

I release my legs' hold around his hips and scoot up under him, moving my back against the arm of the couch. His kisses move down to my collarbone as I wiggle, until he dips his head and kisses my nipples, first the left, then the right.

"Today is a good day." His lips next to my ear feel as warm and soft as they were against my nipples. "One very fine day, indeed."

"Hmmm...." Maybe if I wiggle enough, he won't stop the kisses. Or the tickle strokes he's brushing across my bellybutton. "Yes, one *very* good day."

Dan chuckles but holds himself off me again, planking on the couch as he looks down at my face.

He doesn't speak. His face says it all even though, once again, he's trying to cover it up with the *I'm cool* expression. I see joy and just the right amount of pride. But I also see worry.

"How do we handle this?" he says.

All I want is to take his hand and walk up the stairs to his bed. To sleep for the rest of the night against his side and climb on his cock the moment the sun peeks over the horizon. But he had to ask that question and reality roars back into our world.

And it's not just us anymore.

CHAPTER 7

Daniel

I don't want to move. Seven years with my ex-wife—high school through her pretending to go to college up until my injury—and she never, not once, reacted to me the way Camille does. Not once did she tell me what she needed. Not once did she curl around me the way my angel curls around me now. Not once.

Not once since my injury have I shown a woman my scars. Not any of the three whole dates I've been on. None of them made me feel the way Camille makes me feel.

The way she's made me feel since the strawberry picking field trip. The way I've felt every morning when she greets us at the Community Center and every evening when I pick up Bart.

Not once while I was with my ex, Lori, did I realize wanting to hold a woman, wanting to be close and to kiss and to stay in her—to have her *want* me to stay inside her—was how it should be. Like this. Like it is right now.

With the most beautiful woman I've ever met, much less touched. Who didn't push me away because of how my skin feels. Who, I am pretty sure, likes what I have to offer.

Lori never looked happy during sex. Camille's fingers rub circles across my shoulders and I feel better than I have since the moment I first held Bart. Better maybe, because she'll hold Bart, too.

She kisses my forehead and I don't want this to end. Not tonight. Not tomorrow. I want to wake up with her. To see her in the sun. To love her again like this.

I kiss along her cheekbone, to the bridge of her nose. "How do we handle this?" I whisper. I want her here, with me. I want her here this weekend, when my family comes to celebrate Bart's birthday. *Let me hold your hand while my son blows out his candles*, I think.

Camille presses on my shoulders and I flip onto my back on the couch, taking her with me, my feet propped up on the arm and my angel straddling my hips. She gazes down with her soulful eyes when I pull the throw off the back of the couch and wrap it around her shoulders.

"You've been alone since the accident?" She sweeps a finger across my chest, stopping at the edge of my scars.

I frown. I don't really want to talk about it. What I'd like to do is to put an end to my stunted love life.

So I distract her instead. "You wanna do it again?" I accent my words with a small thrust up with my still-firm cock. She says go and I'll go.

Maybe I shouldn't have shut down this part of my life. But when Bart was a baby, it seemed like the best thing to do. No complications. No explanations about the accident. No pity.

No woman rolling over when we're done, like I don't matter.

Maybe Camille will stay tonight. Maybe she'll sleep next to me, instead of on the far edge of the bed.

I sit up but keep her straddling my lap. The need to distract her from her questions is suddenly subsumed by my own set of questions. About what this means. About "handling" this. About the look of teacherly concern she's giving me right now.

And suddenly I'm wondering if she feels the same strength of connection I feel.

"Hmmmm." But she's biting her lip like she wants to stay. Her hips sway just a little against mine.

I kiss her. It's all I can do. She looks at me with her teacher face and all I want to do is replace it with the ecstasy I saw while we made love. The ecstasy I gave her, and she gave me.

Because it's there. Damn it, it was there.

She sighs and tucks her head into the crook of my neck. Her fingers dance over my scars, touching but not probing. She's careful. Considerate. "How do you feel?" she asks.

Wonderful, I think. But I choose my words carefully. "Half a year of slowly getting to know you and it finally happened." I feel my smile work through all my face—my cheeks and my eyes. My mouth. She's incredibly beautiful.

She blinks. A little shiver runs through her body. And I remember what I said: *I want to be with you.*

I do. But I dance back from the edge of these emotions because I know it's too early to admit they're there, much less talk about them.

"You sound like you planned this." She's grinning. I feel her cheek tighten where she presses her face against my neck.

Plan isn't the right word. Hoped for. Wished would happen. Wanted oh so very much but didn't think possible because, mostly, of that horde of zombie nags inside my head. "I resigned myself to waiting until Bart started kindergarten before asking you out."

I hadn't realized how much I missed having a woman pressed against me. How good soft hips and breasts feel as they rub across the skin of my chest and thighs. How nice a woman smells. Or how calming the sound of her breathing is.

Now I have the loveliest, most caring angel I know caressing my arms with her fingers and I need to be careful or I'll lose the brilliant bit of luck I've got.

So I know I probably shouldn't ask. I probably should see if Tom will watch Bart for a night and ask Camille on a real date. But she's here and she's beyond beautiful. She's wrapped around me and I do not want to be without her. "Stay tonight."

"Oh, Dan," she whispers. For a glorious moment, her arms tighten around my chest, but she pulls away. And sits up. "It's Monday."

"Uh-huh." I grin, palming her sweet breast. It's exactly the right size to hold in one hand and her nipples are little perfect buds. "You are incredible. Blazing hot kind of incredible."

Camille chuckles and looks away, over the back of the couch. "How is this going to affect Bart?"

Nothing would make my son happier than to see his dad with the woman he's taken a liking to. But I don't say it. I don't say *Stay and we'll all talk about it tomorrow over breakfast.*

"I need to be careful." She looks around like she's trying to find her clothes.

Careful? I drop my legs over the side of the couch when she scoots off my lap. "Why?"

She strokes my chest and her fingertips trail over the top of my abs. Her tongue flicks out to wet her lips as if she's considering licking my midsection. I almost flip her on her back again.

"With work. This, with us, isn't against the rules, but I think it's frowned on." Her forehead crinkles. "Some of the other teachers don't seem to like that I'm... sitting for you."

My calm turns to indignation. Why the fuck should they care? Why the fuck should *she* care? It's not like it's interfering with her job. But then I remember: She's new. And not making much. And needs to pay school loans.

My first inclination is to say *Quit. Live with us and quit your job and be here for Bart. And me.* But then I realize what it is that I'm thinking and how caveman it is.

I dance back from this set of emotions too and don't say anything at all.

"I want Bart to be okay," she whispers.

I pull her to my chest and kiss her forehead. My body is screaming *protect* while my brain whirls around in a storm of *what-ifs*. What if she gets fired? What if something goes wrong and Bart can't handle it? What if *I* can't handle it?

"I need to be at work at seven and I don't have a toothbrush here, much less clothes." But she's not moving away.

I have to believe that for once, a part of my life isn't going to degenerate into taking out one lumbering undead must-do after another. That my to-do, must-fight-off unending list of zombies won't invade here, with her.

Monsters that don't die. Monsters that stalk my family with little frowns and admonishments. With the slow wag of a finger because I can't possibly be a good dad and a good lover at the same time. I can't be a man because there's too much that must be done and I don't have the time.

I nod. And I let go.

I don't want to. I just had the best sex of my life with a woman who told me it was good for her too and now we're dancing around emotions and consequences like we made love inside a minefield.

Why the hell can't it be simple for once?

"I think," she says, her face taking on her teacher look again, "that being with you is the best place I can be." She smiles.

For a second, the what-ifs look friendly. Camille, still naked and still beautiful, kisses my chin. "When do you need me next?"

I snort. "Right now." She needs to know the truth of how much having her here means to me, even if reality is crashing down around us. And boxing me in. Again.

She throws me a mock stern look. "To bring home Bart, silly."

She said *bring home*, like she thinks of here as her home. I stroke her shoulder, feeling the silky smoothness of her skin. "Tomorrow." I'll be done by four-thirty and can pick him up early, but I want her here.

"Okay." She kisses me again. "I'll see you in the morning?"

I nod.

"We'll figure it out." She stands up. "I'll bring him home at five and we'll see you soon after?" She's picking up her panties and bra and I want to snatch them from her hands. And carry her upstairs.

I nod instead.

She dresses and we stand together in front of my door, her arms around my waist and mine around hers. She smells sweet and faintly like fruit, and like sex.

And I feel a new herd of zombies creeping up on me—the divorced dad monsters. My brain tosses around every manner of problem it can think of and I see momentary blips of the courtroom. Legal documents. Of car payments and school registration forms.

Why do these things have to invade? Why can't Camille stay and stroke away my tension and let me do the same for her? I'm beginning to wonder if such a thing is possible. Or feasible, no matter how strong the love is.

Camille presses against me and I know, for sure, the strength of what I am feeling. I've been here before. I know. The tingling in my fingers. The very strong desire to touch her all the time. To stroke her skin and ask about her day. The desire to pick her up and set her within the circle of my home.

But I'm not my brother Tom who had nothing to lose by taking a chance and moving a woman into his house right out of the gate. And the woman in my arms has much to lose as well.

Her kiss silences all the real world thoughts, if only for the moment. Her lips feel warm and soft. I want to taste more, to touch more. To see every inch of her skin and to completely map her body. And all her responses.

But she's going home.

"I'll see you in the morning," she says against my lips.

"Tomorrow."

And she's off, gone, leaving me alone in the house I built. I cork the wine and put away the cheese. Standing in the kitchen, alone, I stare at the chocolate in my hand.

She went back to her place. We had sex and she left me alone. But, damn it, I understand why.

My hand tightens around the candy. Understanding doesn't mean I have to like it.

It's not going to happen again.

CHAPTER 8

Camille

This morning, when Dan walks through the Community Center's doors, he's holding Bart's hand. His son skips along with his backpack over his shoulders, trying to keep up, but his daddy is watching the other teachers, not him. Or me.

Dan's stride is tense and borderline belligerent the way I'd expect a man who's about to get into a fight to walk. He wears a light blue button down shirt today, one that's just as wrinkled and uncomfortable looking as all his clothes.

His shoes slap hard against the Center's granite tiles and the sound stops when I walk over. His focus immediately snaps to me and his face softens. "Hi." A small smile lights up his face.

Bart pulls on his hand. He seems happy this morning, bright-eyed and energetic. He's going to be talkative, for sure. "Bye, Daddy." He wants to run off to Sandy's room.

Dan kneels down. "You be good today. Okay, little man?"

Bart nods. "I will!" Then he's off, into Sandy's room, to his cubby.

I step forward a little, so I can see Bart as he hangs his pack on his hook. When I see Sandy acknowledge him, she waves, and I turn back to Dan.

He's less than a foot from me and his gaze is steady on my chest.

"Dan!" I step back, glancing around.

No one seems to have noticed. Dan's bluster is back, but it's not aimed at me. It's clearly aimed outward, toward the world.

"Please don't." I step back again. "We talked about this. We need to be careful. At least for now. Okay?"

He blinks when he looks at my face. His hand twitches as if he wants to take mine, and he frowns. "I don't like it." His lower lip wiggles and I very clearly see where Bart gets his adorable pout.

Chuckling, I would like to take his hand too, but he can't do this. Glancing around again, seeing that it is all clear, I step closer—but not too close—and lower my voice. "You're as spoiled as your son, you know that? And just as cute."

His shoulders relax. The brightness of his smile surprises me. He looks as happy as he did last night, after he told me his good news. And after we had sex.

Absolutely amazing sex. I feel the need to press my thighs together, but I can't do that in the Community Center lobby. And I cannot, at all, be flirting with a parent.

Or have a parent flirt with me.

Still, part of me is kicking myself for leaving. But there are steps to a relationship. And he has a son, so this isn't just about us.

"I want to do this right." I blurt it out the way I swear I blurt out half my words around him. What is he doing to me to make me act this way? It's like my subconscious absolutely *has* to tell him things my conscientious, logical brain thinks I shouldn't. At least not yet.

Dan's lips part but he presses them together as if his logical brain just caught something *he* shouldn't say. Yet.

"It's pizza night tonight." He glances around and stuffs his hands in his pockets. "I downloaded that new kid's movie. The one that's supposed to be funny. Do you want to stay for dinner and watch a little of it with us?"

It's not a date, but I think he's trying. "Are you asking me on a family fun night, Daniel Quidell?"

The grin he gives me is just as swashbuckling and just as devastating as any I've seen from him and I almost melt right here in the lobby. In front of everyone. I want to take his hand and drag him off to the supply closet and kiss my job goodbye for a brilliant quickie with my gorgeous new boyfriend.

Dan nods affirmative, but he suddenly stands up straight. One of the other teachers is watching us from her doorway. Mary Beth. She's not much older than me, and pretty, and had been the most vocal about having Dan take off his shirt during the strawberry picking fieldtrip.

She and I don't get along, though we're cordial. But now I'm wondering. "It'll be good for you to pick him up tonight." We shouldn't be seen leaving at the same time.

Dan nods and points at the door. "Bye, Ms. Frasier," he says loudly, and turns away.

I can't help but watch his perfect backside as he walks toward the door, knowing full well the other teachers can't either, and suddenly I understand Dan's antagonism.

Slowly, I breathe in and out, counting.

There has to be a better way to handle this. Fighting the world won't work. The world always wins.

Bart tells me in full detail about his favorite character in the movie and how Daddy lets him watch half an hour before he has to get ready for bed and how he's going to watch the whole movie on Friday because he doesn't have to take a bath unless he's stinky.

He's been monopolizing my time since I arrived, holding my hand as he takes me around the living room to show me the little scenes he built with his action figures. They all seem to be connected somehow, the scenes, but I'm not quite sure how. He piled all sorts of similar toys at each spot—blocks and markers, a couple of toy cars, and at one, an apple he must have taken from the refrigerator.

"The world needs red!" Bart does a brilliant superhero pose before picking up his favorite figure and running into the kitchen.

So he's saving the colors from the bad guys. I shake my head, knowing I shouldn't be surprised at what Bart comes up with. But sometimes he understands a lot more than he should at his age.

I sip my malbec, feeling it warm my throat, happy that Dan saved the rest of the bottle, as I follow Bart back into the kitchen.

"I like pepperoni." He says it with great certainty, like a young man who has sampled many pizzas and found all other meat and cheese combinations wanting.

I kneel and lean close as if sharing a valuable state secret. "I like pepperoni, too."

Bart presses his fists into his hips and looks up at his father. "I *told* you she would like *my* favorite *better*."

"Bart!" Dan frowns at his boy. "Be polite."

Bart frowns right back at his father and stalks off toward the living room and the line of action figures he set up on the coffee table. He mutters to each in turn, but I can't make out what he's saying.

"I don't know what's gotten into him." Dan watches his son as wipes his hands on a kitchen towel. Absently, he rubs his neck. It must hurt tonight. The oven timer beeps and he nods over his shoulder. "Pizza's ready."

He walks away to prep our dinner before I have a chance to rub away his pain. Out in the living room, Bart bangs his toys on the table, and I'm pretty sure that the Quidell men are fighting over me. But how did Bart figure it out?

I step into the kitchen, where he can't see me. "Did you say something about us to Bart?" I wish Dan had waited until we figured out a game plan.

Dan sets the pizza on top of the stove. "No." His lips bunch up as he gets out a cutter.

I set down my wine. "He's too perceptive for his own good."

Dan snorts. "Just like Rob."

Dan's youngest brother, the one in grad school. From the look on Dan's face, I suspect being "just like Rob" isn't necessarily a good thing.

"Bart is still a little kid, Dan. Which means he doesn't have the vocabulary to express how he feels." Out in the living room, Bart tosses one of his action figures onto the couch. "And I think he doesn't understand sharing me with you. Or you with me. Life has its silos, when you are four."

Dan won't look at me. He doesn't say anything, either. He just kisses my temple and steps out where Bart can see him. "Dinner, little man!"

Bart walks toward us, an action figure in each hand, talking to his make-believe friends more than paying attention to his father.

Dan squats so he's at eye level with his son. He balances on the tips of his toes, his arms resting on his thighs, like he's a superhero watching over a city from the edge of a rooftop.

"Doctor Bartman," he says, one eyebrow cocked. He steeples his hands even though he's still squatting. Dan's doing a Minion One yoga pose.

I don't know why, but it warms my heart. And other parts of my body. He's so incredibly good with Bart. "That hurt your leg?" But he shouldn't be doing it if it hurts.

"Stretches my hips." Dan winks at me.

He's flirting *and* playing with his son. Damn, the man is amazing.

Bart saunters up, his chin up like a good superhero. "Yes?" He presses his fists into his waist.

"There's a grocery bag on the floor next to the shoes." Dan points toward the front door. "Will you get it, please? Before we eat."

Bart's eyes narrow. "Why?"

"Because I got you something special today."

Bart drops his action figures into his daddy's hands and bursts back toward the door as fast as his almost-five-year-old legs will carry him.

"No running in the house!" Dan yells, but he's smiling. When he stands, he runs his hand over the back of his head. "It's silly stuff. I found them in the Christmas clearance bin." His swashbuckling grin reappears.

"What did you get?" I'm as bad as Bart. But Dan's enthusiasm is contagious.

He just grins some more and waits for Bart to reappear.

Bart fishes around inside the plastic and I hear little jingles like he's got a small Santa in there. His face crinkles up when he sees what his fingers found. "Daddy!"

Bart pulls a pair of superhero-covered slipper-socks from the bag. White ones with the knitted-in face of Bart's current favorite hero all over them. Little high bell sounds twinkle off their pointy toes.

Dan bought superhero elf socks.

I try to stifle my laugh but end up almost snorting wine out my nose. Full-bodied South American grapes aren't all that comfortable in the sinuses. I set my glass on the kitchen counter.

Dan's obviously trying not to laugh too, but one escapes when he points at the bag. "Show Camille what else is in there."

Bart frowns and pulls out another pair of superhero elf socks. The second pair is bright green with a different hero face all over them, and are much bigger.

Big enough for Dan. Bart looks shocked.

I can't hold the laughter anymore. I double over, giggling uncontrollably.

"Show her the other pair."

Bart dutifully pulls out the last pair. They're bright red and smaller than Dan's, but bigger than Bart's.

"Are those for me?" Dan bought me hero elf socks, too?

Both Dan and Bart smile the most wonderful, beautiful smiles.

"Does that mean I'm Minion Two?" I'm a Minion.

And it feels better than when I graduated from college. Or when I got my first job. It's as good as the feeling I had after seeing Dan's relief when I offered him help with Bart. It's as good as every hug from every kid at the Community Center.

Bart scratches his head, frowning. "Uncle Tommy is Minion Two." Then he stands up straight and holds out the socks to me. "You will be Minion Two and Uncle Tommy will be Minion Two-Two!"

Dan and I both back into the kitchen counters when we double over laughing.

"Why Two-Two, buddy?" Dan's rubbing at his eye, he's laughing so hard.

"Because I can't take away his job. Uncle Tommy will be sad." Bart sets the jingling heap of socks on the table.

I lean against Dan and press my ear against his big, broad shoulder. He wraps his arm around me, still laughing. Still watching Bart more than me. It's an unconscious gesture and it feels just as right as being Minion Two.

"We should eat before the pizza gets cold." Moving away takes a lot of effort. I'd stay next to him all night like this, if I could.

Which I can. And I think, tonight, maybe I will.

We eat, and Bart seems happy. He chews his pepperoni. After he's in his pajamas and it's time to watch the movie, he plops between us, alternating leaning against Dan and me. By the time we get a half hour into watching the dancing computer-generated animals and their musical numbers, he's already fast asleep against my side, his arm around my waist and his head against my breast.

Dan carries him up to his bed and he hugs his dad the entire way. When I tuck him in, he mumbles something about his birthday and becoming a big boy.

I want to pull him to me and hug him tight. But I place my hand on his back instead, letting this little man sleep.

Dan, holding a handful of action figures, watches me from the door. Quietly, he sets each small protector of the city and the world in a line on Bart's table and they throw a long set of hero shadows onto Bart's pillow.

We close down his door. Dan touches my hand, my elbow, my cheek. We stand in the open space between his son's bedroom door and his own.

The yellow glow of the street light outside filters in through the window over his front door that's visible from the top of the stairs. A long line of bright light falls over each step, and across Dan's feet. Downstairs, the appliances hum. Outside, a neighbor slams a car door. The house smells like pizza and suburbia and...

...and family.

It frightens me. Just a little bit. It feels like the extra stretch—the extra strain—when I stretch my arms too far apart. Like two parts of me want to go in completely different directions.

I open my eyes. Next to me, standing in the open space between his boy's bedroom and his own, is the most luscious man I have ever seen.

Or touched. I feel naughty, looking at the huge, hard male in front of me and thinking about how damned good he feels. How tense and utterly fuckable he is. Because there's a lot more to Dan Quidell than how well he uses his body.

I'm against Dan's broad chest, holding tight, feeling his strength encircle me. How are we going to deal with work and making sure Bart is okay? Dan feels real under my arms—warm and strong and everything I want. He smells like cooking and a long day and I know his shoulder hurts.

All I want to do is to release the pain in his muscles. "I don't want to think about the world or how we—"

His kiss pulls all my worries from my body. He's here—I'm here, with him, in his home. It feels right. I take his hand. And I lead him toward his bedroom.

It's cleaner than I expected, and larger. A king-size bed waits opposite a big window covered with black-out curtains. His dresser lacks the typical man-clutter of combs and wallets and deodorant, though he's got a fabric-covered bin full of random stuff sitting on the floor next to his closet and a basket of what looks like clean clothes. The bed looks freshly made, like he changed the sheets this morning.

Grinning, I stand on my toes to kiss the stubble covering his cheek. "You're wonderful, you know that? Truly wonderful."

The happiness brightening his face reminds me of Bart's joy when he's proud of a drawing. He'll hold it up, his body erect, and loudly declare "Look what I made!"

I have the feeling no one has ever thanked Dan for the little things. For his steady work and his caring.

"I bought jo-jo oil. Or I think it's called jo-jo oil. The clerk at the health food store said it was the best for scars." Dan points at the dresser top. "She said ylang ylang is good too. It smells nice and it reminded me of you, so I bought candles."

Jojoba oil and aromatherapy candles. I pick up one of the pillars and breathe in deeply. The rich, almost jasmine-like scent fills my senses. Ylang ylang carries deep notes that make me hungry, like I smell the preparations of a sweet feast. Not the food itself, but the promise of food. I glance at Dan. And the promise of a great tactile feast.

His skin is a wonder. Yes, his scars pull and rub, but what isn't damaged is healthy and warm and when I touch, I want to touch all of him. I want to taste the saltiness of his stubble and feel the softness of his chest hair. I want to run my fingers over his biceps and watch his face slacken because it makes him feel so, so good.

"Sit down." I motion to the edge of the bed. "And take off the shirt, gorgeous."

Dan curls an arm around my waist and pulls me toward him as he sits. Hands roaming, he stares at my breasts as he strokes my back, my hips, my waist. "Hmmm..." A kiss lands over my heart. "*You're* gorgeous."

"If I'm going to massage your shoulder, you'll need let go of me so I can reach the oil." But I don't want him to let go. I don't ever want him to let go.

"Don't want to." He buries his face in my cleavage. "Have woman."

I can't help but laugh. He's grinning against my breastbone and just knowing he feels good enough to crack jokes brings all my joy to the surface. "Shirt off, man. I don't want your neck locking up during sex and having you fall on top of me. You're *huge* and weigh what? Two-twenty?"

"Two-twenty-eight. I'm down from my full carry-equipment-up-three-flights-of-stairs days."

I moan and my fingers grip his huge arms tighter than I mean to as memories of him holding himself up over me fill my mind's eye.

Dan's eyebrow lifts. "You like?"

I nod, grinning the way he was earlier, like a little kid who just received the best toy *ever*.

"That look is all the motivation a man needs to work out." His kiss steals all my breath.

But he's going to wait because I know his shoulder still hurts.

So I pull away.

CHAPTER 9

Daniel

I light the candles before stripping off my shirt. Her gaze lands on my shoulder scar and for a second I have to fight the need to pull the shirt back on.

But she strokes her hand over my collarbone. "Looks like you might have a knot here." A finger presses on a spot at the base of my neck.

The pressure she applies isn't all that much but I already feel the difference radiating down my arm. "I'm keeping you." Damn it, I am too. She doesn't care about the scars and her touch is magic. And she's the best thing to ever happen to Bart.

When she steps back, I'm entranced by her smile. If I have to beg to get her to stay tonight, I will. I'll drop onto my knees and wrap my arms around her waist and beg like a child.

Though that's probably not a good idea. I smirk, trying not to look too much like a dumbass.

Camille shakes her head. "Now I know where your boy gets his charm."

My smirk turns to a grin and she chuckles as she closes her eyes, breathing in the scent of the candles. I think I made a good choice. She seems to like them. Her body's tension melts away with each deep breath. The candles are a natural beeswax color and they spread a golden glow over my bedroom and over the beautiful woman standing at the foot of my bed.

Just looking at her makes me happy. Seeing the curves of her breasts and hips, and the lines of her jaw and arms.

I reach for her again but she steps back, watching my face, and strips off her blouse and jeans. The bra and panties match again. Some dark red shade. Not that I notice—how they hug the sweep of her hips and push together her breasts is all I care about.

I'm the man who gets to touch the woman in front of me. To kiss and lick and roll her nipples between my tongue and the roof of my mouth. Because she picked me. The angel picked scarred-up old *me*.

It's been too long since I've felt this way. Too long since sex was something available, much less allowed. Camille watches, her face showing the same hunger for me as I feel for her and damn it, it makes me want to throw her down and fuck her blind.

The massage can wait. My cock didn't ease into hardness tonight— it decided the moment Camille pulled me into the bedroom that it wanted her as much as the rest of my body. The pressure from my fly rubs and my entire length aches.

Freeing myself from my trousers and boxers takes a moment and when I pull them off, my cock springs against my lower abs, fully at attention and waiting impatiently for Camille's caresses.

She sighs as she looks me up and down. "Why did I wait six months to kiss you?"

This time when I grab for her waist, she dances out of my grasp and scoops the oil off the dresser. Kneeling on the bed, she points and I sit again. The oil spreads over her palms and she rubs her hands together, warming before she caresses. It smells slightly sweet, like it has a hint of the candles to it.

Leaning back, I press my hips and cock up and pout at her over my shoulder. "I need a massage all over, Ms. Frasier."

Camille responds by nipping the top of my ear. Her teeth flick over my skin, her tongue just touching, and I shiver.

I didn't know the attentions of a woman could be like this. Lori and I started dating young and I never wandered. And after...

Camille's hands move across my shoulders as she nips and the oil between her palms glides like silk over my skin.

...After, I thought no woman would want to take a chance with me. And I put parts of my soul—and my mind and body—in the freezer, thinking I'd never need them again.

Camille's angelic fire is thawing me out.

She rubs gently at first, stroking her hand over the scars, but her fingers probe. She's looking for knots. When she finds one, her thumb presses in and down, forcing the muscle to lengthen along its axis.

Once again, my entire back lets go. I groan, the tingle working down my arms to my fingers, and I turn around on the edge of the bed. Her luscious breasts are right there. Right in front of me, and I yank on her just-covering-her-nipples bra, releasing what I want most.

Camille's head drops back as I tongue first her left nipple, then her right.

"Dan," she breathes, weaving her fingers into my hair.

The desire in her voice makes me harder. So hard my cock aches more than my muscles or my skin. More than the pins in my bones. It pulses to my spine and overrides all the bad pain with good.

I hook my thumbs into her panties and yank them down her thighs where she kneels. I could throw her onto her back and pull them off, but she's insanely sexy with her bra pushed off her nipples and her panties around her knees. Gorgeous and intense.

I drop flat on my back, pausing to take in the splendor of the underside of her breasts. Slowly, she unhooks her bra. Her breasts fall free of the cups, two perfect round wonders of sweet, tender softness, each capped by nipples hard and waiting. For me. For my mouth.

I see the line of her ribcage from this vantage point, and the smooth curve of her belly. Her hips sweep out in perfect proportion to her breasts and I think, for a moment, that I understand what "art" is. What "beauty" means. I'm looking at the underside of its breasts.

She wiggles slightly, inching the panties lower, but I reach over my head and grip her hips. I stroke my thumbs over her hipbones, feeling the smoothness of her body. Slowly, I pull her across the bed. She slides

60

on the sheets, her panties rolling down off her thighs, under her knees and shins. The sheets and the lace crinkle. The sound blends with the popping of the candles on the dresser.

Flickering candle flames aren't the only things blazing right now. So is my woman.

"I want to have sex with you every day." She sounds dreamy. "Every *hour*." She moans as she runs her hands over my arms.

All I know is the sweet, female musk of her pussy. I let go of her hip with one hand. My fingers need to find her clit so I can make her come like I did last night. Now.

She bucks against my hand, slick and pink. Flawless. I lick.

The moan accompanying her full-body shudder makes me wonder if she did, in fact, just come.

Holy shit, I think. She said sometimes it's difficult for her. But the way she responds makes me think I'm doing something right.

I want to fuck her right now. Flip her over and fuck her and make her come while I'm deep inside her. I want to feel her pussy contracting around my shaft. To see her face slack with pleasure.

She drops forward. Her mouth descends onto my cock and the next thing I know I'm pressing against the back of her throat.

I groan into her pussy when she forms a tight seal around my shaft. Her head moves up and down as she vacuums. One of her hands cups my balls as the other holds tight to my hip. I try not to thrust. I try to relax and twirl her clit with my tongue as she works me. But the hand on my hip pulls up each time she takes me deep.

I groan again as I flick my tongue across and around her clit—and Camille quakes as my baritone moves across her pussy. I hum. She sucks and shivers. God, my *voice* gets her off.

Another deep pull on my cock makes *me* shiver. I need to be in her. Now.

I push her up and her mouth comes off my cock with an audible pop. She sits up, still riding my face, and I lick one more time before flipping over fast.

"Did it happen?" I need to know. Damn, this is amazing.

Her tongue traces her lips. "Yes," she breathes, her eyes closing. "God, Dan, *yes*."

I throw her down on the pillows and yank on her hips as she drops. Her ass is on my thighs before she hits, her legs spread and pussy open, her mouth slack.

"Do it hard like you did it last night. Pound me." She pinches her nipples, rubbing her breasts, urging me to fuck her.

I scoop my strong arm under her hips and pull her toward me as I guide my cock into her opening with my other. I'm in, deep, and I feel her clench around me. She's tight and hot and slick. I pull almost all the way out before thrusting again.

"Is it always going to be this good?" I'm barely able to ask the question.

A guttural moan erupts from Camille when I bottom out, hitting her deepest parts, and I can't go deeper.

"Hold my wrists." She lifts her arms and crosses her hands in front of her face, the insides of her wrists pressing together.

I'll have to let go of her hips. But she asked.

I wrap my hand around the top of her clasped fingers. Leaning a little forward, I hold her ass on my thighs with my other hand, and continue to pound into her.

"Lower. Around my wrists. Squeeze." Her mouth is open and she's breathing hard.

Damn it, I don't want to have to think about balancing while I'm fucking.

I must have made a face because she pulls back her hands and pinches her nipples again. "Keep doing what you're doing." It bursts out of her fast, between two thrusts. "*Ah...*"

I can't talk any more. But I can finger her while I pound her senseless. Carefully, I find what I want, and jitter the pad of my thumb against her clit.

A loud, high-pitched yelp rolls out of her throat.

Fuck yeah, I think. I lean forward and take my weight on my arms. I want to *feel* her yell. My kiss quells the next yelp and Camille laughs against my mouth.

I pound her hard. She rocks with me, clenching her abs as I slide in and out, tightening her already unbelievable pussy. My balls slap against her ass and my whole body feels just as heavy and tender.

My orgasm is like the rush after the sting of a pinch or the pulling off of a bandage. Every nerve in my body makes a brilliant cocktail of endorphins and chemicals and fires a lightning storm through my senses. I *hear* my cock releasing. I swear I'm bathed in fire.

She locks her legs around my waist and refuses to let me move off her, even though I weigh two-twenty-eight. I'm still inside her and it's wonderful. Beautiful. My Camille smiles and strokes my cheek and, I think, for the first time since the accident, I fully relax.

"You seem happy." Camille kisses my shoulder. "Feel better?"

She lets go enough I can roll off, but I take her with me, pulling her close, keeping her tight against my body. Her forehead feels warm against my neck, but her fingers feel cool when she runs them through my chest hair.

I pull her hand to my lips and gently kiss each of her knuckles, one at a time. "A lot better."

I feel her smile against my skin.

"Did you come a second time when you yelled?" I want her to feel as good as she makes me feel. Better, if I can.

"Almost." She twirls her fingers in my chest hair. "You are amazing."

Part of me can't help but feel a little miffed. I don't have practice with women other than my ex and Camille but I should be better than "almost." And what kind of sex is she having if "almost" is "amazing?"

"I'll do better next time." I pull the sheet and blanket up and cuddle with her, inside the warmth.

Camille chuckles but doesn't say anything.

"Will you stay?" I whisper. She'll need to go to work in the morning but I have to ask. "I'll set the alarm early. We'll eat toaster pastries and all go to the Community Center together."

Camille smiles and gently kisses my lips. "Toaster pastries?"

I'm about ready to do the begging I know I shouldn't. "Bart will be okay. We have all week to talk about it. Rob flies in Thursday night and Bart's party is Sunday. He'll be fine by then."

My arms tighten around her even though I should probably give her space, but I can't. "You taking an interest in teaching him, and helping us, and..." I close my eyes.

I feel Camille push up on her elbow. She doesn't say anything.

When I open my eyes, she's watching me carefully. Like I'm going to break. "I think you've been alone too long," she whispers.

Shit, flits through my head. What am I doing? Am I scaring her? For the first time in my life I'm in a good relationship and all I want is to make it real.

"Dan." Camille kisses me as gently as I had kissed her hand. "I brought my toothbrush."

She's staying. She's going to sleep here, with me. I'm going to wake up tomorrow and she's going to be here and we'll get it all squared away with Bart.

I touch her face. I don't remember moving my hand but she's kissing my palm and I'm happier than I should be.

"Sometimes," she says as she lays her head on my shoulder again, "I wonder about your ex. About how she treated you and Bart." She looks up again. "I read the file."

I close my eyes again. My calm starts to drain away and the zombies start massing. Lori is the last person I want to talk about.

"It's okay." Camille kisses my cheek. "I'm sorry I said anything."

"No, no." I roll on my side and force away the unease. That part of my life is done. Lori's gone and she's never coming back. "I'd rather talk about you."

Camille and I are flush against each other, chest to chest, belly to belly. She scoots closer and wiggles a leg between mine. It's beautiful and warm and better than any time with my ex.

Every time with my ex.

Camille kisses my chest. "You're going to be like this all the time, aren't you? Asking me to stay."

Until you move in, I think. "Uh-huh."

"Because you want wake-up sex. Admit it." She strokes my chest again.

I feel how much Camille cares in how she strokes my arm. In how she cuddles against me. She's perfect and I don't think before I open my mouth. I don't censor myself or hold it back because this is right. I hold her close and kiss her hair and what I feel rolls out of my mouth. "Are you promising me a morning of passion with the woman I love?"

Camille stiffens. Right here, right now, in my arms, she stiffens like she's gone cold. Her heart speeds up and pounds against my chest and she's not looking at me. Not doing anything.

And I feel the slush return to my veins. I'm cold again and I can't move fast enough to get away from the zombies.

"Dan..."

Why did I open my mouth? It slipped out.

"Dan!" She kisses me. Not the sexy, horny kisses of earlier. This one's different. It's slow and her lips press against mine but it's sweet. And it's distant. "You *have* been alone too long."

I snort. It should have been a laugh or a chuckle or some sort of suave noise but no, I flat out snort like a St. Bernard.

Camille sits up. Her teacher face returns and she watches me for a long moment. I can't tell what she's feeling. I've never been able to read women well. If I could, I would have ended it with Lori before she killed our marriage.

But I can tell what Camille is about to say.

"I don't think I should stay tonight."

I totally fucked up. Work's been good. The kid's good. I have an incredible girlfriend and I just fucked it up because I'm lonely.

I might as well admit it. *Lonely* is me and I am it. And it looks like we're going to continue to be conjoined, lonely and me. Together, always.

I should have kept my mouth shut.

"I think we need to slow down, that's all." She kisses me all sweet and distant again. "*You* need to be sure. We both need to be sure. For Bart, at least."

I nod. I want to throw the pillow at the window and rip down the curtains. Get dressed and go for a run and punch a brick wall some-where. Go into the basement and lift until my elbows pop and every muscle in my body burns.

I need to find some way to get a little heat back into my veins.

"I am not breaking up with you, Daniel Quidell."

I glance at Camille. I know she's assessing my mood and that she thinks I'm acting like a little kid. That, right now, I'm no better than Bart was at dinner, when he stomped off.

Maybe she's right.

Her brow pinches together and I swear she's going to poke her fists into her waist the way Bart does when he's mad. "Say something."

"I'm sorry?" What the hell else am I supposed to say?

She swings her feet over the side of the bed. A small shiver runs up her spine when she turns her back to me. I hear a sigh, too. A small one, like she's trying to be strong.

Not picking her up and pulling her back into the bed takes all my concentration. I don't think about what she's saying. I see only that she's upset.

"Camille..." Gently, I touch her back. She feels cool again, like the air pumped out by the furnace isn't keeping her warm. Like she needs to be against me.

Her back straightens but she doesn't turn around. "You know, I do like toaster pastries. The blueberry kind without the extra icing."

Why did I have to scare her like that? "Bart likes cherry."

She glances over her shoulder. "I'll see you tomorrow morning?"

I nod. I'm an idiot.

Camille gathers her clothes. The candlelight flickers over her lovely skin, the heat crackling, and I can't help but wonder if I'm dreaming. If, perhaps, my brain has had enough of my six months of wanting to be near her and I've finally snapped. If the last few days have been a dream meant to force myself into admitting I'm in love.

And that, perhaps, I moved too *slow*, after the field trip. That by *not* asking her out I signaled I wasn't serious.

So now I have to think about it. Be sure. Because if I was sure, I would have figured it out before the leaves fell from the trees and the slush moved into the world.

I roll off the side of the bed and pull on my clothes and follow her down the stairs to the living room.

She stands in front of the door for a long moment, her bag in her hand and her knit cap pulled down over her ears, ready for the cold outside. The house buzzes and clicks, reminding me how empty it's going to feel the moment she walks out my door. But she thinks I need to think, so there's not much I can do about it.

At least tonight.

Camille digs around inside her bag. Smiling, she pulls out another, smaller bag. It's bright green and quilted and, I suspect, holds her toothbrush. "Will you put this in the bathroom upstairs for me?"

I take the little bag. My fingers wrap around the scratching, polyester fabric, and I feel little bottles and brushes move around inside. "I'll clean out a drawer." Grinning, I set the bag on the steps, so I remember to take it up.

When I turn around, she hugs me tight, and the pom-pom on her hat brushes against my chin. It tickles and a shiver flows across my jaw.

"I'll see you in the morning." The shiver is followed by a kiss. A sweet, warm kiss from a woman who's leaving her toothbrush here, but not sleeping in my bed.

I nod and let go.

"You're quiet." She grasps the door handle but doesn't open the door. She just watches me with her teacher eyes.

If I start talking, she'll run away. Probably forever. "I don't know what to say."

Camille looks at her feet. "We'll talk tomorrow. Make a plan. Okay?"

I want to kiss her. I want to pick her up and carry her back up the stairs and go to sleep happy for once in my life. Happy and feeling like I conquered the zombies instead of them eating my limbs while I watched.

But not tonight.

When she leaves, I watch from the window until I see her headlights vanish around the corner. I'll see her in the morning.

And I'll have a plan. Because I'm going to fix my mistakes. I may have taken it too slow before, and too fast now, but starting tomorrow, it'll be just right.

CHAPTER 10

Camille

Dan and Bart are late this morning. I pace in the Community Center lobby under the bright skylight, listening to the kids yell and the front desk staff laugh and smelling the bad coffee they brew every morning for the gym crowd. What if I scared Dan away last night? What if he thinks I'm some kind of ice queen or something?

I *had* to leave. I had to. I had to pull on my clothes and pick up my bag and walk out the front door. I didn't have a choice.

That teenaged part of my brain screamed *Yes!* when he said "the woman I love." I wanted to pull Dan on top of me and kiss him deeply and watch his beautiful eyes light up with all that joy he shows when we're together.

I feel it in his fingers. In the way he touches. I taste it in his kisses. I hear it in the smoothness of his voice. He's not lying.

Dan Quidell loves me.

But another part of my head was screaming *What did that bitch do to him?* What, exactly, did his ex-wife do that made him so lonely?

Because I don't think it was anyone else. He hasn't said, but I think I might be the first woman he's been with since his divorce.

Which means I'm the rebound. I pace again inside the big white glare thrown through the skylight. I'll need to go in soon. All the other kids are here. Everyone but Bart.

I pull out my phone. Should I call?

But how can I be the rebound if it's been almost six years? What if he's *settling*?

When I close my eyes, I see orange and green after images from my phone. And from the pool of sunlight. Maybe from all my fretting.

How the hell did Dan go with no girlfriend for six years? Hot, handsome, fun Dan?

Sandy ducks her head out of her room. "You okay?"

I stop pacing. "Bart's not here."

She opens and closes her mouth, but doesn't say anything. She just nods before returning to her room.

Shit, I think, careful not to say it out loud. At work, I try not to even think swear words, in case one slips out, but sometimes it's difficult.

I know why Dan's gone for so long without a girlfriend. The surgeries. The scars. And, I think, expectations. Men like Dan—gorgeous men—are expected to be interested in only sex. I know how the other teachers react when he's around.

That's not Dan.

And he's in love with *me*.

I'm smiling. I'm fretting but I'm smiling. But I won't admit how I feel. I won't do anything that, in the long run, causes him pain. I won't let him charge headlong into a relationship because he *does* deserve all the respect I can give him.

And if I admit it to myself, I'll jump into his arms when he finally does come through those doors.

And he'll sweep me up into his big, strong arms.

Maybe I should.

No. Both Dan and Bart need rational, not weird and fawning. He needs to be sure.

The doors swoosh open and I look up from my phone's screen. Dan strolls in carrying a big, flat box, Bart next to him.

Bart immediately runs for me and the next thing I know, he's hugging my legs. "We're going to the zoo on Thursday! Do you want to go to the zoo? Daddy says you can come. I want you to come, too."

I stuff my phone in my pocket as Dan walks up. He's in a t-shirt and his work boots, so he must have a more hands-on day ahead. The t-shirt hangs loose around his midsection but its long sleeves do nothing to disguise his biceps.

A sudden ping of jealousy—or maybe it's possessiveness—flits through my gut and I glance over my shoulder, making sure none of the other teachers are watching my man. It happens so fast I surprise myself.

When I glance back at Dan, he's watching me with a raised eyebrow. "No toaster pastries at the donut shop." But he smiles and nods to the box.

"Is that why you're late?" The box is full of every kind of donuty goodness the shop has to offer. The sweet smell of sugar and fat leaks out every time Dan jostles it, too.

The cocked eyebrow turns into a frown. "We wanted to get you a peace offering."

"You didn't need to do that." I touch his elbow before I realize I probably shouldn't out here in the open, but I don't think I care anymore. We may need to be careful and slow and rational, but seeing him frown makes me rash, fast, and decidedly irrational. "I was worried."

Dan blinks. "Oh. Sorry." He looks like he's about to drop the box and lift me up for a good strong kiss. One of his mesmerizingly intense lip massages that, by themselves, are so damned good I almost come.

Because I want to be with him that much.

Bart tugs on my shirt. "Are you coming to the zoo? Please?"

"Thursday is your day off." Dan shifts the donuts to his other hand. "Rob's flight comes in at five so I thought we could go to the zoo during the day and then I'll pick up Minion Three while the little man here gets his pajamas on. That is, if you can stay for a while on Thursday evening. I'd like to introduce you to Rob."

I work ten hour days four days a week, with Thursdays and the weekends off. "You don't have meetings on Thursday?" He's been working so hard, though. He needs a day off.

"Moved them. Tom's gallery opening is next Tuesday so I thought I should concentrate on what's important for a couple of days." Dan musses Bart's hair but he's looking right at me.

I see worry flash across his face, like he's afraid that the time off will catch up with him and bite him in the ass. Or that his peace offering won't be accepted.

"Please, Ms. Frasier!" Bart tugs on my shirt again.

"Bart, what did I say in the truck?" When I look back at Dan's face, I can tell he's counting as he breathes out. That all this—Bart begging, him doing his best to present himself as a cool and calm boyfriend bearing gifts, the party this weekend, his youngest brother coming into town—is stressful. I don't think he has a lot of reserves to dealing with it all.

Frowning, Bart looks up at his father. "Be respectful."

"Are you being respectful?"

Bart tugs on the straps of his superhero backpack and stomps his foot. "I was asking!"

I tap Bart's shoulder and point to Sandy's room. "Why don't you go on into Ms. Cunningham's room so I can talk to your daddy, okay? We'll get it all figured out."

He huffs but does as I say, scuffling across the concrete floor.

"My first pull-out is in a couple of minutes so I don't have a lot of time." I reach for the donuts. "I'll put these in the break room."

"I know it's not a date but Tom can't really help right now because of his show so I thought maybe spending the day with both of us would be okay."

I tuck my hand under the donut box, intending to lift it from Dan's grip. But our fingers touch. We stand for a second, fingertip to fingertip, and the electricity flashes through my body again. It curls from my knuckles to my wrist and all the way up my arm. The tingle touches my shoulder the way his lips touch my skin. It strokes my back the way he kisses my spine.

And under the box, I sneak my hand into his. "You're worrying too much again."

We stand for a moment, palm flush against palm, a box of sugary treats balanced over our wrists. Dan smiles. And I see some of the stress drain away.

"I'm sorry if I came on too strong last night." Dan glances around. "I just—"

He stops talking when I squeeze his hand. Carefully, I let go and take the box. "What time should I be at your place Thursday morning?"

Dan blinks and I see more of the stress drain away. "We could pick you up."

They could. "I'd like to have my car."

He pouts more than frowns. "Oh."

"So there's a car at your place when you're picking up your brother." I shake my head. "You *do* worry too much."

His pirate smirk appears and he tucks his hands into his pockets. "If you're over by nine, we can be at the zoo by ten."

"Okay." The Community Center's big clock dings. "I gotta go." I don't think. I just do. I lean close and kiss his cheek.

Dan opens his mouth to say something but slams it shut and steps back. "Bye, Ms. Frasier."

Blinking, still smiling, he rubs the back of his head as he walks away, toward the door.

When I turn around I see why he responded the way he did. Mary Beth is standing in her door with my morning pull-out students, frowning.

CHAPTER 11

Daniel

Bart's bouncing like one of the prairie dogs in the exhibit along the Northern Trail. "I'm cold."

We rode the monorail over the outdoor animals but Bart wanted to see the tigers up close. At first, he was too excited to notice the temperature, but now that he's seen the tigers, he wants to go inside.

I swing him up into my arms. "We're almost there, buddy."

Camille rubs her hands together and her breath curls around her face like a little cloud. The day smells clean and fresh, and we pretty much have the run of the place, except for the many wandering groups of school kids.

The trail loops through the trees and we walk along, listening to the other kids and the calls of the zoo's many birds as we make our way back to the main building.

Camille rubs Bart's back when he leans his head against my shoulder. He's excited, but he's also beginning to tire.

"Do you still want to see the fish?" she asks. "It's warm and you can rest."

"Oh!" Bart bounces in my arms again.

"Hold still, buddy. I'm carrying you, here." He's going to be too big pretty soon. He's already almost too big for Camille.

Bart ignores me and bounces anyway. "Will we see sharks? I want to see a shark."

"We'll see sharks." Camille pulled her hair into a ponytail today. Her face looked different this morning when I opened the door and it took me a while to figure out that she's not wearing make-up. I just thought she looked fresh and dewy. Her skin glows more.

She tasted fresh, too, when I kissed her in the kitchen. A little like coffee, but clean, like the winter air. I think I like make-up free.

All I want to do is lay on the couch with her snuggled in next to me. Spend the day kissing and making love. Breathing in her scent and tasting her skin. Letting her presence center my mind and her body soothe my aches. But she wants to do this right.

Which is wise.

But I'm as impatient as my son. And I have a plan.

We did the trails first, focusing on the tigers and the giraffes. I gave Bart my phone and he snapped pictures until he was satisfied, so he has "references for his drawings." He sounds just like his Uncle Tommy when he says it.

When we hit the Tropics Trail, he strips off his coat but he still wants to be carried. The brightly colored birds chirp and the komodo dragons flick their tails, but more than anything, I think Bart wants to sit on the carpeted step in front of the zoo's big aquarium wall.

It's a long, dark hallway down to see the fish. I set Bart down and he skips along ahead of us, his excitement returning. "How many sharks are there? Can we get a shark, Daddy? I want a shark."

Camille leans her head against my shoulder. "I suspect he'll be drawing sharks for at least three weeks."

"Fluffy kitty-sharks with tabby markings." I weave my fingers through hers as we walk.

The aquarium wall is a good fifty feet long and at least ten tall. Bart presses his nose against the glass and watches the fish swim by. Camille snaps a few photos of him with her phone while I sit on the carpeted step behind where he camps out.

My hip hurts. I think Bart might have to walk for a while. I rub at it absently, watching Bart point at all the little fish.

Camille sits next to me, enjoying a rest while my son enjoys the exhibit. It smells like aquarium water and people in here, but we're mostly alone, at least for the moment.

When she leans against my shoulder, I wrap my arm around her waist. She wiggles closer. For a second, I wonder if I can sneak a real kiss, but I behave like a gentleman and weave my fingers into hers again instead.

It's quiet here. No random group of fourth graders around.

I think now is the time to put my plan into action.

"I've been thinking a lot about what you said." I have been, too. "About moving too fast and doing this right."

Camille doesn't pull away. She snuggles closer. "Oh?"

In front of us, Bart's mesmerized by a shark that's taken up position directly in front of him. The blues of the water play over his face and hand, and when he laughs, it mixes with the piped-in sounds of the water lapping against the glass.

"I want to explain myself." Give some perspective. "I decided last night to give you a reason why I said what I said."

Telling her how I feel is telling her the truth. I have too many lumbering nag zombies and thinking about how every single word I say may be screwing up my relationship is just making them bite harder.

So I suppose I'm being selfish.

Bart laughs and splays his fingers over the glass. He's not tapping, which means at least he's listening to Camille's instructions, even if I'm not. I'm done thinking about it. I splay my fingers over her hip.

But a small part of me is frowning and stomping his feet because I never get to be selfish and maybe this once I can because this is something important.

Camille is important. Extremely important.

She moves so she can see my face better.

Even in the low blue glow of the aquarium, I see her attentiveness. All her focus is on me, except for the little constant bit she keeps on Bart.

"For the past six months, I *have* been planning. Every morning, I plan what to ask you about when I drop off Bart. Every evening, when I pick him up, I plan a follow up question. Because I've been trying to get to know you."

I grin and sniff. "Though you're good at redirecting and getting me to talk about myself."

Camille grins, too. Gently, she draws little circles on my thigh with her finger. "You're interesting." She leans against my shoulder again. "I never thought about fire prevention and structural engineering issues before."

"I've learned a lot about you." I kiss her temple. "And each piece of information I gathered made me want to be with you more than I did the day before."

Against my shoulder, she inhales sharply and I can't help but pull her closer. We sit huddled together on the scratchy zoo carpet, watching Bart watch the fish. And, I hope, solidifying what I should have tried to solidify months ago.

I breathe in the scent of her hair. "I know when your birthday is. I know your favorite color and your favorite flower. And I know you want to visit France someday." *Maybe that someday will be our honeymoon,* I think. "Plus a lot more I'm not going to say right now."

"Daddy!" Bart stands up and points into the tank. "A diver!"

I look up. They must be feeding the sharks.

I pull my arm out from around Camille. "I guess it's time to take more pictures."

"How do you know all that?" She looks confused.

Chuckling, I nod toward my boy. "Doctor Bartman likes to talk about his favorite teacher. Something I wholeheartedly encourage."

Her mouth opens and closes as we stand. I pull my phone out of my pocket.

"I just don't want you to feel like you're..." Her lips thin and she twists to move to Bart's side.

I grip my phone, hoping I made sense. "Feel like I'm what, Camille?"

She blinks, but looks up at my face. "I want you to be *sure*, not just settling for any old relationship. You deserve better than that."

"You think I'm settling for *you*?" I don't know how else to describe how I'm feeling other than shocked. Flat out stunned and shocked.

Because she's stunning in every way a woman can be stunning. "I thought you were settling for *me*."

I think, maybe, I embarrassed her a bit. She won't look at me but she's smiling.

But I can't help but joke. "You know, since I'm 'almost amazing.'"

"Dan!" Camille throws me one of her mock-stern looks. "My mom taught me to never settle for less than the best."

I kiss her gently before snapping a picture of the woman I am in no way "settling" for. Sometimes I can't believe how beautiful she is.

Or that she's my girlfriend.

When we leave, Bart walks between us holding both our hands. He talks nonstop about the diver and the sharks and the tigers he saw earlier. Camille smiles the entire time.

And I think she's glowing more than she was before.

We have lunch and hit the gift shop before heading home. Bart falls asleep in his booster seat but is wide awake by the time we pull into the garage, chatting about the animals and his new zoo toys and insisting that he's going to wear his new zoo-themed pajamas for Uncle Robby.

"Can we have pizza tonight?" Bart stands in the middle of the kitchen and stuffs a cookie in his mouth as he asks.

Camille shoos him toward the table. "Sit down while you eat your snack."

He nods and climbs up onto his chair, his cookie in one hand and a juice box in the other.

I pull Camille close and kiss her cheek. Bart watches like it's the most normal thing in the world. "I think he's okay with this. With us."

She nods, watching him more than me. The kiss she gives me is warm and wonderful and I feel that maybe we're okay. That we're moving in the direction we need to move.

And maybe she's seeing me as a man who has already gotten to know her. Maybe I'm no longer conjoined with *lonely*.

"Go get your brother." Camille kisses me again. "We'll be here when you get back."

CHAPTER 12

Daniel

I'm going to introduce Camille to Rob tonight. I'll introduce her to Tom and his fiancé, Sammie, at Bart's birthday party. Maybe a little of Sammie will rub off on Camille. Sammie was living with Tom a week after they met.

I can only hope.

I smile to myself and tap my steering wheel. Tom's always been better with women than me. He handled his relationship with Sammie well right from the beginning. Unlike me.

Still, Camille seems to have forgiven me.

Rob, on the other hand, is a little shit. It's not his fault. Our mom and sister's deaths did a number on him. It did a number on *all* of us, me included. Rob is smart enough he should have figured out that he's a little shit and stopped his shitty behavior a long time ago. But he's managed, somehow, to continue in his ways through college and now, I bet, at his new graduate school.

I inch down the freeway toward the airport to retrieve my shit of a brother for a weekend home. He can't stay for Tom's opening even though it's Tuesday. He's got a midterm. But we're going to video chat it for him and Bart's excited.

I've seen some of the paintings my middle brother is showing. We had a talk about Bart seeing naked ladies, especially when the naked lady is Sammie. But we have a plan, and Bart is so excited he's drawing special pictures for his special no-nudes corner of the gallery.

The truck slowly moves along and I watch the brake lights in front of me flash on and off. Rob's waiting by the airport pick-up doors and texting me every five minutes asking where I am.

Driving, I text back, which I do when traffic stops. *Stop texting me you idiot.*

My little brother is an impatient brat.

If my brothers and I are the Norse superheroes in Bart's action figure collection, Rob is the skinny, dark-haired, evil one. The clever evil one. He's way too smart for his own good.

But I love my brother. He reminds me of our mother.

When I pull up to the gate, Rob tosses his bag into the back of my truck before climbing into the passenger seat. He looks as bohemian as most college students—stubble, worn clothes, but with expensive earphones around his neck and the latest must-have phone in his hand.

"You smell like coffee," I say.

He pulls across his seatbelt and settles in. "Love you too, asshole. About time you showed up."

I give him the finger.

Rob laughs. "Someone needs to get laid."

I snort and pull the truck into the traffic lane. At this rate, it'll be nine by the time we get home and Bart will be in bed already. And I won't have any time with Camille.

"Well, well." Rob's eyebrow arches. "How long you been banging the nanny?"

I glare at him. How the hell did he figure out I was in a relationship with Camille? Then again, she's the only woman I talk about. "Do *not* make her feel uncomfortable."

Rob throws his hands into the air. "Sorry. Not going well?" He pulls out his phone and swipes at it a couple of times.

"It's going just fine. You taking notes?" He might be. He's always aware of the shit going on around everyone. He likes figuring out social systems the way normal people like to solve puzzles. Which is why he's in graduate school and I'm walking around with my high school diploma and a few college courses under my belt.

"Of course. I'm trying to figure out how you and Tom attract the hotties." He glances over before shoving the phone back into his pocket. "And manage to keep them around."

Except my ex-wife had issues I was too stupid to see at the time and my new hottie wants to take it slow.

Rob puts on his best mocking face. "Turn that frown upside down, young man, before we get back to your place. The boy's going to wonder what his uncle did to his daddy." Rob nods to the traffic. "It's going to be all Uncle Robby! Uncle Robby! Daddy's fucking my nanny and I want a puppy!"

I roll my eyes. But I can't help but chuckle. "He wants a kitten, not a puppy."

Rob laughs. "Tom said something about Bart taking a shine to his girlfriend's cat." He takes out his phone again. "That woman is freakin' hot. How the hell did he get her to move in with him after knowing her for what, a week? Two? I need to learn his secrets." Rob swipes again, then tucks away the device. "Research purposes only. God knows I don't want a woman leaving her yogurt in my fridge and her tampons in my bathroom."

"Tom and I are going to step back and watch the ladies snip off your balls." Traffic's loosened and I turn onto the main north-south artery. Looks like we'll be making good time after all. Which is just fine. My brother is an annoying little shit.

Now Rob gives me the finger. But his voice drops low when he speaks again. "They're serious, aren't they? Tom and Sammie?"

I glance over. His face has that faraway look he gets sometimes when he goes all wistful. "He gave her a ring, didn't he?" A bright little sapphire because, for some reason, indigo holds a special meaning for them.

They have an ease to their relationship I hope to build with Camille.

Rob asks about Bart and tells me about his classes as we drive home, obviously not wanting to talk about women anymore. I have him text the pizza place and put in an order for dinner, and that seems to shut him up.

Though I can't shake the feeling my smartass little brother has something on his mind.

☙❧

CAMILLE AND BART ARE COLORING AT THE KITCHEN TABLE WHEN WE come in. Bart's in his zoo pajamas, all clean and ready for bed—and also wearing his new Christmas socks. He screeches and jingles his way to his uncle, and I set the pizzas on the kitchen counter.

Camille watches Rob for a long moment, her deep eyes searching. She smiles but I can tell she doesn't know what to do.

She's wearing her Christmas socks.

My first instinct is to scoop her up and lay a massive kiss on her perfect lips right here, for my brother and my son to see. But I don't want to embarrass her, so I squeeze her fingers instead.

Before Rob sets down Bart, he gives Camille a friendly hug, smiling too, but doesn't say anything other than pleasantries and comments about the jingle toes when Bart does a little dance.

Over dinner, Camille quizzes Rob about school and his studies.

"Cultural Anthropology." Rob sits back in his chair and takes a sip of his beer, watching Camille. "I will be job-free and homeless the day I finish my dissertation." He winks at me. "Guess it'll be me living in your basement instead of Tom."

Bart points at his uncle. "Uncle Tommy makes better mac and cheese!" Then he leans toward Camille. "Ms. Frasier makes the *best* mac and cheese."

Rob gives me one of his *oh, boy* expressions but all I want to do is crawl over the table and lean against Camille, too. When I feel her toe stroke my shin under the table, I smile.

"Dan tells me you enjoy French cooking." Rob whistles at Bart and directs him back to eating his pizza.

"My parents gave me a new cookbook for Christmas." Camille and Rob drop into a long conversation about France and French culture.

Bart bounces in his chair and holds up his foot. "Are there super-heroes in France?"

Camille laughs and rubs his hair. "Maybe you should ask your uncle. He knows all about all the different places in the world."

Bart grins as he stuffs his pepperoni and extra cheese pizza in his mouth, quiet now that his mouth is full.

Rob drinks his beer, watching.

After dinner, Rob takes Bart into the living room. "Show me your army, buddy." He winks at me over his shoulder.

Camille chuckles. I pull her into the kitchen.

"Hmmm..." I hoist her off the floor, my arms under her sweet back-side, and set her on the kitchen counter. "Looks like we get a moment."

Up on the counter, she's close to eye-to-eye with me. She bounces her slippered feet. Her heels tap the cabinet door making rhythmic *thump twinkle thump twinkle* sounds.

It's unbelievably sexy. Or maybe it's the luscious pout she's giving me. I don't know. But I think I want moments like this to keep happening.

"You know something?" Camille strokes a finger across my chest. "I like being with you. I like talking to you. I even like your brother." She glances around me and listens to Rob and Bart playing in the living room. "He's funny and good with Bart."

"Hmmm..." I'm too busy kissing up her neck to her earlobe to pay all that much attention.

Smiling, she kisses my cheek. "It's not just the incredible sex."

There's genuine caring in her eyes. It's as deep as the caring I see when she looks at Bart. Different, though, but I don't know how.

I move close, curling my arms around her waist, feeling this beautiful woman and her wonderful, soothing touch. "Will you stay tonight?" I kiss her neck, her jaw. "Rob's not a problem." The next kiss I lay on her lips. She tastes fresh, even though we just ate. "Please."

Concern works across her cheeks. "Don't you want time with your brother? I don't want to be in the way."

"Daddy!" Bart runs into the kitchen waving a piece of paper in his hand. "I drew Uncle Robby's ph—"

My son stops cold when he sees my arms around Camille and I can't tell if he's shocked or happy.

But then he runs for us, his arms wide. "Hugs!" he yells, and jumps for us both.

Camille jumps down and laughs when I lift him high, kissing his cheek.

Bart snuggles in close. "I like hugs."

"I like hugs, too," she says. She watches me as she says it, not my son. Me.

And all I want to do is pull them both close. Kiss them both. But my brother is watching from the dining area.

Camille kisses my lips this time. "I'll get him ready for bed." She walks past Rob, nodding once, and disappears around the corner with Bart. "Story first, buddy?" I hear her say, then the sounds of Bart pulling books off the shelf under the DVD player.

Rob watches them until I hear them settle into the couch. I drop a plate into the dishwasher.

My brother walks into the kitchen. "When's the wedding?"

Out in the living room, Camille reads Bart a story. He reads along, sounding out words. She's going to have him reading novels before he starts kindergarten.

"Tom and Sammie are thinking late spring." I drop another plate in the dishwasher. "I told him they should go to Vegas."

Rob looks me up and down and rolls his eyes as he pulls a beer out of the fridge. He's looking at the floor and not me. Then my brother suddenly smiles and slaps his leg. "Women are impossible."

This isn't about Tom and Sammie. Or about me and Camille. "You were a douchebag to a woman again, weren't you? What's her name?"

Rob sniffs but doesn't answer my question. I peer down the hallway. Bart's drawing a picture of Camille on the big pad of paper thrown over his bright green kid's-easel. She's sitting on the edge of the couch, both her legs to one side and her chin up, like she's a mermaid.

My son stands tall and sticks up his thumb, peering around it at the woman who is better to him than, I think, even me. Who is better to *me* than I am to me. Wonderful, caring Camille.

But what if it doesn't work out? What if I end up more like Rob than Tom? Bart couldn't handle it if he lost her.

I tap the kitchen counter. Bart would be devastated.

Rob watches me watch them. "That bitch Lori is gone and your arms and legs work." He takes a pull on the bottle. "I like Camille. I suspect Tom will as well."

Rob shakes his head. "Dad always says the best thing you can do for a son is to love his mother." He snorts and takes one last sip.

But the sadness hasn't left Rob's face and I *know* this isn't about my delicate sensibilities. "You didn't do anything illegal, did you?"

Rob blinks and his eyes narrow. "You are pathetic, you know that?" He shakes his head as he drops his empty into the recycling. "You're like a goddamned puppy, the way you look at her."

With that, my brother walks away, into the living room.

After a long second, I hear Camille laugh and Bart fuss about brushing his teeth and I lean against the sink, wondering what it is that has me worried.

Because I'm not like Rob. I'll do all the necessary work needed to hold together my relationship.

CHAPTER 13

Camille

The streetlight in front of Dan's house buzzes in the cold evening air. Snow floats down, the crinkly kind, and tiny sparkling ice crystals pelt the world. Somewhere down the street, a dog barks. My boots crunch through the crust of the new snow and my breath hazes the air between me and my car door.

It's time to go home.

Not because I want to. Dan asked me to stay but I told him he needs time with his family. And me time to get used to what happened today.

Not so much the speed, because Dan's right. We've known each other long enough for a serious relationship. But today, at the zoo, it dawned on me that I am, in fact, in a serious relationship. With the man I've wanted for half a year.

Somewhere deep inside, a part of me doesn't think it's real.

Dan doesn't think I have demon eyes. And he's fun. And responsible. And damned hot.

I allow myself a full, deep sigh, out here in the cold, my car keys in my hand and my breath curling around my face.

I hear the front door. Rob had been sitting on the couch when I pulled my coat out of the closet. Dan stood next to me, first looking at his brother, then at me, then back to his brother.

Rob, for his part, gave Dan a "you're a fucking idiot" eye roll and went back to watching some awful reality television show on some random awful channel, a beer in one hand and his phone in the other.

I had expected Dan to plop on the couch next to his brother, not follow me outside, but he dashes down the steps, careful of the snow. When he stops, he zips his jacket and stuffs his hands in his pockets. "It's cold tonight."

"It is." I yank the flaps of my hat low over my ears. "What time should I be here for the party?"

Dan blinks his gorgeous eyes and they look more silver—like the snow—than their usual ocean-like blue-green. I'm in the presence of Jack Frost, except this Mr. Frost only looks cold because he burns with a blue flame.

His pirate smirk flickers for a second and I know what he's thinking: *Right now. Come back inside.* "Tom and Sammie will be here at noon."

I nod. "I'll text before I come." Stepping close, I give him a quick kiss. "I'll see you tomorrow."

"Meeting you was the best thing that has ever happened to me. And to Bart." He waves at the house and again I see what he wants to say in his eyes.

"Oh, Dan." I wrap my arms around his chest and lay my cheek over his heart. The zipper of his jacket rubs my skin but it doesn't matter. I'm safe in the arms of this wonderful man.

"After you leave, the house feels wrong. Because you're missing." He rubs his face against the knit of my hat.

When I look up, his eyes say everything.

The words we've been circling around, the words I should *not* say now because we're being rational and taking the correct amount of time, just pop out of my mouth like they have a life of their own.

And I just say it. "Are you asking me to spend the night with the man I love?"

I say it.

The shock on Dan's face quickly turns into the bright, intense joy I saw the first time we made love. He lifts me high, even on the snow, and his kiss steals all my fears. It warms all the cold shivering my bones. And it convinces me that he loves me as much as I love him.

"Come inside. Please." I barely hear him, he's kissing me so deeply. His next kiss is as strong and as wonderful as the first.

I can't go back to my silent apartment. Not after admitting how I feel. I pull him toward the house.

I'm in his arms again, kissing his jaw and neck. We fall through the door, laughing and touching, Dan stroking my arms and my shoulders. His fingers grip, but gently, and his eyes all but gleam silver in the evening's light.

And completely unaware of Rob until he throws a pillow at Dan's head.

"Get a room, you crazy kids." Fake frowning at us, Rob turns off the television. "I'm going to bed so keep it down."

Leaning against Dan's shoulder, I watch the youngest Quidell brother whistle as he strolls toward the lower level, leaving us alone.

Dan weaves the fingers of both his hands around mine and tugs me up the stairs. He walks backward two steps above me, his grand and obvious erection right there in front of my eyes.

Oh, the wonders of this man. Of his smile. His touch. And his kiss-able wondrous abs.

The look on his face shows half concern over what we *should* do—sit down on the steps and talk—and what he so very obviously *wants* to do—be naughty. Right here. Because I'm staying and he doesn't have to worry about asking again.

Which half do I indulge? Which kind of assertive should I be?

I run my finger over the bulge in his pants. The fabric of his jeans feels thick and taut, like what's under it. Dan closes his eyes and his face turns toward the ceiling. A low, stifled moan makes it past his tightly closed lips. The fingers of his hand grip the handrail and the wood creaks under the pressure. His other hand splays over the wall, palm flat. If he's not careful, he'll poke his fingers through the wallboard.

I glance over my shoulder, listening for Rob. I hear him shuffle around in the lower level, then the click of a door as he goes into the guest room to sleep.

Dan, too, glances over his shoulder, listening. Making sure Bart's asleep. When he looks back at me, he's grinning again.

"You have no idea what your pirate smirk does to me," I whisper.

He blinks for half a second, but then he exaggerates his grin and leans closer. "So I be pillaging ye tonight, aye?" he whispers back.

I'm tingling. I run my hands over my breasts and down between my thighs, squeezing and pinching my own flesh. Playful Dan makes me want to suck his cock right here. Right now.

The pirate grin changes into Dan's look of raw hunger. Backlit by the light over the steps, I see the outline of his shoulders. His muscles contract and his arms just get bigger and harder. I could rub myself against his bicep and come a thousand times.

The handrail groans again, and this time, so does the wall. Dan mouths two words: *Do it*. The electricity fires through my body, brought on by the intensity of his face alone.

You gonna pound me? I mouth, though I know the answer. I like it when he borders on losing control and he's slamming me with all the strength of his incredible body.

His eyes narrow and another low growl makes it past his closed lips. *Arrgh, matey*.

A snort I can't stifle bursts out and Dan laughs, doing his best to stifle his own sounds. He totally blocks the stairs with his big body, not moving, not reaching for me or grabbing my hair or doing anything... planned. But that's not quite the right word. More like expected of him. He got beyond "ask Camille to stay" on his evening checklist and I rewarded him for his hard work by telling him the truth of how I feel. And now he wants to play.

He's happy. Carefree, I think, for the first time since I met him.

I watch his face slacken as I rub my palm over his cock. He looks as if the simple act of touching him solves all the world's problems and seeing his joy makes me happy, too. Happy and horny as hell.

I loosen his belt, working carefully and as quietly as possible. He glances up the stairs again, then twists his head, also listening for Rob. When he's satisfied, he gives me a quick nod.

I undo his fly, slowly unzipping his jeans, more to tease than to keep quiet. Impatience hums off his body and I'm surprised he doesn't make the stairs groan from the vibrations. I half expect the walls to bow out from the sheer pressure of his desire alone.

All his heat focuses on me. "Aye, the mast is up, me lovely pirate lady," he whispers, winking while he exaggerates his grin again.

"You going to tie me to it, good sir?" Now might be a good night to introduce some of the naughty tricks I've learned. I don't think he's got toys, but we can improvise.

Keeping quiet's going to be difficult, I'm certain.

I work my fingers into the fly of his boxers and rub my thumb and forefinger up and down his shaft as I loosen the button.

His body quakes under my touch, his cock solid and hot in my hand. I haven't released him yet. Haven't worked him through the fly of his boxers. I grip him under the fabric and run my thumb up and down the underside of his shaft.

"You be a fierce and terrible creature, one brimmin' with the fire of angels." His lip curls and I see on his face what he's not saying: *Suck me already*.

I twist my hand around and stroke his balls. The quake turns into a shiver and his hand comes off the wall. Dan grabs my ponytail, curling my hair around his hand, and stares down at me.

The fabric of his boxers pulls and stretches as I lift the elastic waistband over the head of his cock, down his shaft, and under his balls. It's not comfortable. I can tell by his grimace. But it should heighten the pleasure of the experience.

I run the pad of my thumb over the head of his cock, spreading a bead of pre-cum. Dan tastes not-quite-salty. Not sweet, either. I don't think it's a flavor, but it is hard and living and hot. He feels so very good in my mouth.

I feel his hips wanting to buck. He wants to thrust. I suck hard, pulling him deeper with only the force of my throat.

"God damn." Dan's voice is smoky, deep, barely capable of making words.

I pull off him but I keep my hand around his shaft. "Are you going to give as good as you get, pirate man?"

He swings around me, rubbing his cock against my breasts as he moves to the steps below. Roughly, he grabs my ass and pushes me up the stairs. His other hand works under my shirt as we move, under the band of my bra, and around my breast. Having his wrist between my bra and my skin makes the elastic dig into my ribcage but the sting only intensifies the pleasure when he pinches my nipple.

The hand on my ass moves between my legs as he pushes me up the stairs. He turns his palm sideways like he's making a gun, thumb up and pointer finger extended, and rubs my pussy. Behind me, he uses his teeth to pull up my shirt.

At the top of the stairs, he pushes me down on the landing, belly to the floor and ass hanging over the first step. The hand on my breast pulls out of my bra. The band snaps hard and I moan. Dan chuckles as both his hands work my jeans, unbuttoning, unzipping, and yanking them down my hips to my knees.

I'm wearing a sweet pink boy-cut thong tonight. One with a wide band of lace around my hips but not a lot else. The growl it elicits from Dan is loud enough Rob probably heard it downstairs. I don't think Dan cares anymore.

He bends over me, his knees outside mine on the first step. He grips the handrail and his shoulder pulls back, but I feel the weight of his body. And his hard cock against the cleft of my ass. "Hmmm, fair maiden," he whispers in my ear. "You bring nothing but joy to this pirate's heart."

His fingers grind into my ass and he pulls away enough to maneuver his cock into the tight space between my denim-constricted thighs. "So I will offer you a boon. Fucked..." He thrusts against the outside of my pussy, his cock rubbing over the just-barely-there lace. "... or licked." A finger follows his thrust.

Dan very quickly, expertly, finds my clit.

My growl is as loud as his.

"Bedroom, bedroom, bedroom," I beg. We need to shut the door. I can't be quiet. God, not with him.

Dan hoists my legs onto the landing and I crawl across the floor, my jeans around my knees and his fingers in my pussy, into the bedroom. The door swings shut fast, about to slam, but Dan catches it and carefully pushes until the latch clicks.

I stretch up, still on my knees, and yank my top over my head. Dan presses me against the wall behind the door before I can unhook my bra and his mouth latches onto the nape of my neck. The full length of his hard body presses against my back. His cock rubs fire hot against the curve of my lower back and his hand moves down my belly, under the lace around my hips.

Slowly, his fingers work into my pussy. "You haven't answered."

I can't. I can barely breathe. His pointer finger rubs my clit and his middle and ring fingers circle around my opening. He can't do much more, with my jeans around my knees.

I move his free hand to my breast. "Pinch." Just the little extra should be enough.

Dan yanks down the cup of my bra and flicks my nipple like he's flicking away a bug.

The orgasm shudders through my belly and down into my thighs with lightning speed. It thunders into my breasts and across my nipples, up into my neck and throat and to the spot just below my ear where Dan breathes on my skin. A loud whimper flows from me and my muscles lose their cohesion. I flop backward, against Dan's front, and every inch of my body chimes.

A *heh* finds my ear. He's proud of himself.

"Pillaging pirate," I moan.

He undoes the clasp on my bra and pushes the straps off my shoulders, kissing each inch of skin the elastic slides off of. "I'm happy you're staying."

Behind me, he pulls off his t-shirt. I feel his hard abs against my back, his hard cock against my ass. Slowly, he lifts me to standing, but he keeps my jeans where they are, on the floor. I step out of the fabric, feeling his hands roam over my hips. Feeling his fingers hook into the lace of my panties and pull them down, too. I stand naked, still facing the wall, listening to Dan remove his jeans and his boxers.

I close my eyes, seeing in my mind the perfection of the man behind me. His balance. His strength. The wonder of his healthy skin and his intense, focused need for me. The curve of his cock and the tightening of his neck muscles that happens every time I stroke him with a firm grip.

Dan spins me around.

CHAPTER 14

Daniel

I'm not greedy. I don't demand, but I need her kiss. My tongue dances into her mouth, then darts back. Hers traces the outside of my teeth.

I cup her breasts, one in each hand, and massage with great care. My thumbs rub her nipples and I swear I feel the tingling heat she feels. I swear it fires into my hand and up my arm. I can only hope I make her feel this good. The way she makes me feel.

Her neck tastes sweet. Fresh, like the rest of her. She moans and I lift her off the floor, arms under her backside, and hold her high enough I need to tip back my head to kiss her again.

Camille curls her arms around my head, kissing my lips and my forehead. Her fingers trace my ears, touch my temples. Her hands stroke my neck.

Our gazes lock. I hold her in the air for a long moment, watching the desire and the love in her eyes. It's there. For me. And I kiss her again.

I slide one foot back, then the other, until we reach the bed. My hands move on her sweet round ass and my forearms tense. Her weight feels good on my muscles. My back, my chest, my arms all tighten, all ready to respond.

I widen her legs.

Camille wiggles, helping my cock find her opening. When I sit on the edge of the bed, I thrust all the way in.

"Oh my God," she breathes. She's straddling my lap, riding my cock. I grip her hips, to keep her from sliding off. And to work her tight pussy up and down my shaft.

I move slow, or else I'll be in a frenzy. She's set my entire body on fire, and I want it to last.

I lift up until I'm almost completely out, then down again until I'm buried deep. "Do that clenching thing you do," I whisper. Her pussy contracts and changes shape and I don't pretend to understand, but it's something only an angel can do.

She tightens her lower abs as I pull her up. "Like that?"

It's magic. Hot, smooth, bright-white magic wrapped around my cock and pulsing into my abdomen and my chest. And all the way up into my head.

I groan, my eyes half closed. "Jesus, Camille." I slide her down and she circles her hips.

She can't leave. Not anymore. Something new opened between us tonight and it's weaving itself through my entire body, up my spine, into my legs. It's knitting me back together.

It's as if I physically feel the net she's made for me, to stop me if I fall. Camille's here now and I won't drown in the cold slush.

I want to give it back to her. Make the same intensity, the same connection, and do it right so she'll always understand.

"Tomorrow." I pull her up, moving faster than before. "I'm going to love you in the morning. In the sun."

Every morning, before we go to work. I'm going to do this again with her lips pressed against my neck and her breasts against my chest. Feel this with her, knowing she's here.

"Dan." She plants her knees along my thighs and takes some of the task, pumping on me.

Up, then down, I slide in, then out. Each time, I fill her farther, deeper. How can she do this to me? How can she be so intense, so exacting, and make every fiber of my body quake?

I loosen my grip on her hips and I roam my hands over her ass, her back. I kiss her breasts, her neck, knowing my breath is as hot and as demanding as my cock.

But I need to say it as much as I need to feel it. And my arms tighten around her waist.

I press my face against her collarbone. "I love you."

I love this magnificent woman.

"I love you, too." She whispers her words into my ear and her full-body, bright-white angelfire takes over.

I flip her on her back. I use my thumb on her clit like I did before, but this time I don't think about what I'm doing. Not pumping takes all my concentration, but I want to feel her come before me. While I'm on the edge and buried inside her.

I circle my hips so that the head of my cock hits every point inside Camille I think will make her scream. Her eyes roll back and I kiss her, taking into my mouth her loud, stuttered moan.

My spine doesn't know if it should arch or curl when my abs flutter like I'm swimming. But I'm not drowning. I breathe in rhythm with the woman under me and this is right. With her it's right.

She's here. She's given me back my strength and I don't feel the weight of the world anymore.

I can't finger her anymore. I can't be slow. I lean into her, kissing her again, and pound her so hard she slides upward on the bed. Our bodies hit and the mattress groans, but I don't care. Her fire is burning away the slush in my veins.

When I come, the world blanks out. I see only her beautiful eyes and hear only her heart beating, and it's perfect.

Camille curls her fingers around mine. "Hmm, pirate man, you plunder well."

I try not to laugh but she smiles. She's righted the ship of my life. I kiss her gently, dancing my lips across her cheeks and her chin. With one hand, I caress her shoulder. With the forearm of the other, I hold myself up. "Did it happen twice this time?" I'm going to make it happen.

"Almost." She wiggles but doesn't move out from under me.

"Almost?" Again? I frown.

"I tell the kids all the time that it's good to have goals." Camille's eyes look brighter than usual. "Almost" must not be all that bad. She wisps her fingers over my lower back.

The tickle makes me wiggle. I forget my irritation.

"I'll bring over my toys." Another wisp of her fingers makes me chuckle.

I slowly lower myself as I kiss her neck and shoulders. "Hmm..." At this point, sleep is more interesting than talk of "toys."

My life's coming together. I have all I need: A beautiful girlfriend who cares about me. A company that's doing well. And a brilliant son who loves her as much as I do.

I roll off. We cuddle under the blankets, wrapped around each other. She rests with her head on my shoulder and runs her finger through my chest hair.

"That tickles." But it feels good. *She* feels good.

"You know I'm going to have to go back to my place sometime tomorrow. I need clean clothes. And to get the toys." Absently, she runs her hand over my scarred shoulder.

I kiss her forehead. It doesn't matter. She'll be here in the morning.

And tonight, I sleep well.

CHAPTER 15

Camille

I straighten my blouse and ponytail when I hear the doorbell. Today is my first encounter with Tom and Sammie. Dan said she models for most of Tom's paintings and I can't help but feel intimidated.

Dan's ex was model-worthy, too. The Quidell men seem to like their woman beautiful.

It's dumb, I know. But I did have a guy tell me I have demon eyes.

Bart pulls me toward the front door. "Uncle Tommy is here!"

When Dan swings open the door, Bart lunges for his uncle. "Did you bring me a present? Uncle Robby brought me a present but he won't let me open it and it's small." He scrunches up his face. "Did you bring Mr. Pickles?"

Tom hoists up his nephew and strides through the door, doing the same duck and twist Dan does when crossing thresholds. He's not quite as tall, but he's just as broad, with lighter hair and the same brilliant blue-green eyes.

"Kitties don't like the cold, remember?" Tom winks at his nephew.

Bart frowns. "I remember. I want a kitty. And a shark!" He thrusts his fists into his waist again.

"Shark?" Tom grins and offers me his big, beefy hand. "Tom. Sammie's coming with the little man's birthday tribute." He nods over his shoulder. "You must be Camille."

I shake, standing as tall as I can. "Nice to meet you."

Behind us, Rob helps Sammie with a big package and a few smaller ones, and I immediately see why Tom paints so many pictures of her. She's taller than me, with auburn hair and striking eyes. But it's how she walks, and how she watches the world, that telegraphs her assuredness. Capturing her composure would make any painting special.

Dan takes Bart's birthday haul and sets it against the coffee table, with Bart's other gifts. The rest of the afternoon is a whirlwind of family stories, birthday cake, and the tearing of gift wrap. Three new superhero costumes from Dan, a special pad of artist's paper from Tom and Sammie, a new action figure playset from me, soon rest as a giant heap of Bart-ness on the coffee table.

Bart's favorite, at least for the afternoon, is Rob's gift of a special little kid's camera. It downloads wirelessly to Dan's tablet computer. Bart strides through the house with the camera strap looped around his wrist, taking picture after picture, while Dan and Rob follow behind holding the tablet so Bart can instantly see his work.

I spend much of the time chatting with Sammie, asking questions about Tom's show. She has an entrepreneurial streak and when I mention that Dan could use some help her eyes light up. The next thing I know, she sits Tom and Dan down to discuss logos and business plans.

When the doorbell rings, Dan and Tom are deep into "company branding" and I pat Dan's arm. "I'll get it."

He squeezes my fingers and kisses my cheek. "Thanks, honey."

I like being in an official relationship. As I walk to the door, I think I like it so much I might bring up moving in some of my clothes. And maybe my easel, so Bart and I can paint together on the weekends.

I peer through the peephole and see only the back of a woman's head. Expecting a charity looking for donations, or someone wanting to share their faith, I pull open the door, ready to politely send her on her way.

But I recognize her the same moment the winter chill hits my face. Blonde, taller than me, ice blue eyes. Gorgeous. I see why the teenaged Dan fell for her.

My first reaction is to step outside even though I'm in my t-shirt. Even though the night is chilly. But this woman cannot see Bart and Bart cannot see her. I close the door, leaving only a gap wide enough for me to slip my arm through if I need to.

The former Mrs. Quidell wears a nice but thin blouse under her open leather jacket, and I see her glaringly yellow camisole. Her hair is swept up into a loose but smooth ponytail. And she grasps the handles of a bright, clown-themed gift bag with expensive looking gloves.

"I have a gift for Bartholomew." She holds out the bag. The laughing clown design is appropriate for a toddler, not a five-year-old boy with art and superhero fixations. "Is he here?"

My gut tightens up so much I want to throw-up, but I don't show it. Why would she appear now? Like this? But it's obvious. She means to passive-aggressively cause as many problems for the Quidell family as she can.

I don't answer. Instead, I glance past the door into the living room, hoping to catch someone's eye. Situations like this are best handled by two people, for reports and support.

Dan says something about "angelfire in the logo" and I hear Sammie's clear, high approval. Then Rob's warm baritone rolls through the house. But none of them are close enough to see me.

I look Lori Taylor-Quidell straight in the eye. "You need to leave. If you wish contact, this isn't the time or place to do it." She's non-custodial and Dan told me she needs written permission from him and a social worker, as well as supervision, to see her son.

I shiver and rub my elbows. I won't let this woman near Bart. Or Dan. I think talking about his ex-wife drags up memories he doesn't want to re-experience. Dan and Bart don't need her ruining the evening. Defusing this situation without raising alarms is something I can do for them.

I hear Rob again. He sounds closer, so I quickly duck my head through the door.

He's sauntering toward the stairs, his phone in his hands and his eyes glued to the screen.

"Rob!"

He looks up.

"I need a witness to back me up."

Immediately, he sees who stands on the front step and his surprise turns to anger. I watch his shoulders take on the same tense hardness Dan's do when he's upset and Rob's stride also takes on the same semi-belligerent swagger.

Rob swings open the door and very quickly steps between me and Dan's ex. He doesn't ask or acknowledge that I have this under control, or that I asked him to show support, not to take over.

He's not as big and broad as Dan or Tom, but he's still taller than most men, and he easily blocks my view of the other woman. I see him swipe something on his phone.

"State your reason for violating the terms of the divorce and custody trials, Lori." Rob's recording her every move.

"I don't give you permission to have that thing on!" From around Rob's shoulder I see Lori's shocked expression.

"Dan gave me blanket permission to film on his property for all reasons I deem valid, including but not limited to matters of security." Rob sounds like a cop. He's authoritative and dispassionate, the way you're supposed to respond to a potentially threatening individual.

He shifts when I do, to stay between us. "Camille, as the other witness here, do you give me permission to film this event?" He holds his phone over his shoulder so it picks up my face.

"Yes, I do," I say into the phone's camera. At least we will have documentation.

"Thank you." Rob returns to holding the phone so Lori is squarely in the center of the frame.

Lori's face hardens. She holds out the gift bag again. "I have a birthday gift for my son."

He's not your son, I think. *He's Dan's son and he's much better off because of it.*

"The terms of the custody agreement clearly state that you are not to be within three hundred feet of Bart without the permission of a social worker and the child's father. You do not have that permission today."

Rob holds the phone over his shoulder again. "Camille, are you aware of any attempt by this woman to contact Dan?"

"No," I say, as clearly as possible.

"How the hell would *she* know?" Lori points a finger at my face.

Rob shifts again and completely cuts off all sightlines between us. "You are well within the three hundred foot limit. You leave *now*, Lori."

"Is she fucking him? In the same house with *my child*?" She screeches the last two words.

I hear rustling. Tom yells something from inside. Chairs scrape and I hear Dan hand Bart over to Sammie.

Rob takes a step toward Lori. "Camille, please dial 911."

Jabbing her finger at his phone, Lori backs down the steps. "You can't use that in court, you goddamned ape! I don't give you permission!"

I slide the screen on my phone so it lights up and hold it out, for Lori to see.

"Go inside, Camille." Rob waves his hand over his shoulder. "Keep Dan away."

I step back into the doorframe.

Tom appears first. "What—" His face turns the same hard, angry menace I just witnessed from Rob and he pushes by me, out onto the step. "Shit."

Lori drops the bag on the concrete of the walk and fumbles open the door of her rental. Rob immediately snaps photos of the car and the license plate. When she gives him the finger, he snaps a photo of that, too.

Like Rob, Tom looms between me and the car, a giant mountain of male protectiveness. Why do they both act like I can't handle myself? I'm trained for situations like this.

The door swings fully open and Dan pulls me into the house. "Why is she back?" His tension hums off his muscles and his face turns hard and cold.

Tom glances over his shoulder and his brows knit together when he sees the anxiety on his brother's face. "Stay inside, Dan. We've got this."

Rob picks up the bag and walks toward the house when Lori pulls out of the driveway.

The cold finally bites into my skin and I shiver, rubbing my arms. "I didn't need either of you blocking her from me."

Rob glances at Tom before looking at Dan. His eyes narrow just like Tom's, and he fiddles with the video he just took.

Tom nods, looking me up and down. "Sorry. Reflex. But you be careful around her."

Dan wraps his arms around me as I step into the warmth of the living room. "I could have handled her." He tenses again and his arms tighten around my waist.

"It's Bart's birthday. You don't need her shit today any more than he does." Tom pushes by.

Rob stands in the door for a moment, watching the street. "Camille, did you call the cops?"

Dan's watching Rob over my shoulder. "Did she threaten Bart again?"

I didn't call the cops. I only held up my phone. "I haven't called yet."

Dan turns me around. His grip on my arms is strong enough it actually hurts. "Did she threaten *you?*"

I read the file. Lori Taylor-Quidell threatened to steal Bart when the custody hearing came back in Dan's favor. The judge responded by restricting her contact to supervised visits, and only with specific permission.

Then she disappeared out West, with a new boyfriend. Dan hasn't seen her for two and half years.

Until today. "Is she violent?" The file only says she is non-custodial with no contact.

Dan glances at Rob again. "Someone vandalized Rob's car when he was an undergraduate. No proof it was her."

Tom paces and rubs the top of his head with his hand. "I had items stolen. A music player. A laptop. Again, no proof."

Dan lets go. "Goddamn it." He steps away. "I'll call the non-emergency number. We need to file a report."

When he and Tom walk away, Rob holds the door. "I'm sorry I offended you earlier." He nods toward the street.

Down the hall, Sammie works with Bart at the dining room table. She's pointing at something he's drawing. He laughs, happy, and holds out the paper for her to see.

Rob stops next to my side. He glances down with eyes clear of all the menace I saw earlier. "I know *her*. She fucked with Dan's head pretty bad when he was at his lowest, lying in his hospital bed hopped up on pain meds. Told him everything that happened was his fault because he's boring and can't make good decisions."

"He believed her?" I glance down the hall as Dan dials the land line.

Rob sniffs. "She ripped at him the entire time they were married, but in small ways. Saying things Tom and I didn't realize were causing him pain. That stuff accumulates."

He watches the street for a moment, then shuts the door. "I think the stealing and the damage was revenge on Tom and me because we won't let her near Dan anymore."

"Will she come back?" My gut reaction of keeping her away from Dan was right. He doesn't need to see her again. That part of his life is done.

Rob swipes at his phone. "Maybe. Her tolerance for work is low, even working at making someone else's life hell, so I don't know."

I squeeze his arm. "Thank you."

Rob scratches the top of his head in very much the same way Dan does when he's perplexed. "Just be alert, okay? I'll be damned if she causes harm to the only woman who has ever given my brother joy."

Nodding once, not looking me in the eye, Robert Quidell walks away, toward his family.

CHAPTER 16

Daniel

Bart became quite excited when the cops showed up to his birthday party—once I explained that nothing bad happened, just that Daddy and Uncle Rob needed to report an unwanted visitor.

Uncle Tommy had already cleaned him up and gotten him into his pajamas when the two officers pulled up in their cruisers. Bart stood in the front window watching, his eyes wide and his mouth an open circle, as the officers looked over the front entrance area and the driveway.

When the younger officer, a squat kid with a military buzz cut, waved at my son before his partner came inside, Bart all but wet his jammies. So Sammie bundled him up and carried him out to see the cop cars, three of his superhero action figures gripped tightly in his mittens.

The officer who waved let him sit in the back after taking a minute to play with him and his toys before he, too, came inside.

Bart asked his new friend if he could take a photo with his birthday camera so he could draw a good picture. The young officer set his hat on his hair stubble and did a fine cop pose. I got his email, promising to send him a copy of the picture when it's done.

At least my son had the good type of "memorable" evening. Me, I'm fidgeting. I want to pace. But reports need filing. So reports get filed.

The older officer, a tiny woman with a graying ponytail named McMillian, talked with everyone one at a time, starting with Camille. When Rob took his place at the table, he hooked his phone to the cruiser's laptop and downloaded the video. When my turn came, I handed Bart over to Camille. His excitement had worn off and he tried very hard not to suck his thumb.

Camille squeezes my fingers before carrying him toward his room. "Time for bed, little man."

"Two and a half years?" Officer McMillian asks me.

"Yes. She vanished without leaving a forwarding address or phone number." I had hoped we'd never see her again.

When Camille walks away, McMillian returns her gaze to her laptop. But she doesn't ask another question right away. "I remember when you were injured. I remember all the hoopla, too. You doing okay now?"

I nod. The support the city gave me—and in particular the police and my station house—was what got me through my injuries and my court battles. For a while, when Bart was an infant and before Tom moved in, six police and firefighter families cooked my meals and helped care for my son.

But that all stopped when my therapy dropped from "recovery" to "maintenance."

"It's good. I have a big contract with a hotel chain." I lean back in my chair, smiling.

McMillian nods. "Good. You don't need any more shit. So let's do a thorough job documenting, here."

She taps at her laptop. "Your brothers both seem to think she's caused damage to their property in the past. Do you believe this as well?"

"Yes. No proof, though. No charges." I look over my shoulder. Tom and Sammie speak to the other officer as they prepare to leave. His gallery show opens on Tuesday and they still need to stop by the space tonight.

I wave. "We're all taking extra precautions."

McMillian nods. "Did you see the incident on the front step?"

"I was in the kitchen." Camille had tried to spare me from facing my psycho ex. I feel a frown try to harden my face, but I fight it.

On the one hand, I'm thankful. And thrilled she handled it as if she's part of the family. But on the other, I'm terrified Lori might come after her.

After a few more questions, McMillian closes her laptop. "We're done here." Her little portable printer spits out a hard copy of the report. She also transfers an electronic copy to a thumb drive for me. "I suggest you inform your son's school immediately that his birth mother is in town."

"I will."

Camille turns the corner, having come back down the stairs. Bart must be asleep.

"My girlfriend is one of the teachers at the Community Center. She's there all day," I say.

McMillian sets all her police-issued electronics into their case and closes the lid. For a long moment, she watches Camille. "Several of us do security work up there on our off hours. I'll get the word out."

We shake hands when she stands. "Thank you."

After she leaves, I still want to pace. I still want to throw shit at the walls and punch a hole in a door. I can hold it together when the cops are around.

But McMillian's gone.

And that bitch Lori poked her nose back into my life.

Why can't I calm down? But I know why. This is Lori's M.O. Hurt in small ways then run off and let it fester.

Still, I won't take the chance that she might come back tonight. I stand with Camille in the front entrance for a long moment, holding her tightly against my front. "I don't think you should go back to your apartment at all this evening." I want her here, where I know she's safe. "I know you can handle yourself, but I'd feel better if you didn't go."

"I need a few things." But she nods against my chest. "Will you come with me? Follow behind. We can fit a lot of my stuff into your truck."

She's more than staying tonight. I think, maybe, she wants, at least partially, to move in.

With me. With Bart. My happiness must be obvious because she's smiling, too.

"Don't get a big head, pirate man. We still have a lot to talk about." Camille reaches for her bag.

From the kitchen, Rob raises a glass of water in salute. "I'm not going anywhere. Until tomorrow." He shrugs and walks toward the television. Picking up the remote, he clicks it on and drops his ass on my couch. Using his full arm, he clears an open area in Bart's accumulated toys, and props his feet up on my coffee table.

Camille weaves her fingers into mine and pulls me toward the door.

CHAPTER 17

Daniel

Camille's apartment is a cramped space with rickety windows and worn, cheap carpet. The building smells faintly of old deep-fry grease, and the paint in the hallway to her apartment has a sticky texture.

I don't like it. I tap along the hallway wall, listening for the studs. It should have cinderblock firewalls between every other unit at a minimum, but the building looks—and sounds—hollow. Even with the old fire codes, the inspector should have done a better job.

"This place is a deathtrap." I sniff and tap the worn door to her apartment. It's thinner than it should be and sounds filled as opposed to solid. There's a gap under it, as well. One perfect for drafting in smoke.

I can't tell if she's amused by my statement or annoyed. Either way, she's out of here tonight.

"The rent's cheap." She pushes her key into the lock and wiggles it because it sticks. When she pushes it open, I follow her inside.

Like most apartments, hers has a galley kitchen off a small living area and a bath and bedroom off a short hallway. I feel a cold breeze moving through the room from the windows over her couch. I bet they whistle when it's windy.

"What's your lease say about giving notice?" The less rent she needs to pay, the faster we can pay off her school loans.

She doesn't have a lot of stuff. The furniture we can sell or put downstairs. I have room for all the books. And I've already had an artist living with me, so I know where to set up her easel downstairs.

We can have her out of here by Monday morning.

Camille drops her keys on her kitchen counter and turns slowly. "Sounds like someone's made up his mind about what he wants."

I've made some shitty decisions in my life. Marrying Lori, for one. Not sticking with college. But Bart's happy and I think that even with our rocky start, I'm doing well with Camille.

Lori showing up isn't going to ruin what we're building. I won't let it. I've got a good thing going.

And all those to-do zombies? For the first time in my life, I feel like I have them under control.

That my actions won't breed more.

"I don't want to waste any more time."

Camille watches my face the entire time I step toward her, but she doesn't look upset. Or annoyed. And I think maybe she's made up her mind, too.

"I wasted six months because I didn't know what to do." I used to worry about what Lori wanted. Was I making enough money? Were my brothers okay? Someone had to pay attention.

But I don't feel that way with Camille. I feel like she's got my back. Like my decisions are right.

Slowly, she runs her finger over my belly. "I think you knew what to do. I think you just didn't trust yourself to do it."

I'm in her arms before she finishes her sentence. Up close, her subtle yet sweet scent fills my senses and I want to rub my palm over her breasts. It's as if my brain recognizes the few moments alone we have and immediately wants to take advantage.

"Rob told me how she used to tear you down."

I blink, my attention pulled away from thoughts of nibbling on her nipples. "I don't want to talk about Lori." I'm done thinking about my ex. I wrap my hands around Camille's waist to pull her closer. We're in a child-free environment.

And I suddenly very much want to lift her onto the counter and fuck her right here, in her kitchen. Slowly. With her beautiful eyes lighting up with joy and pleasure. With her lips on my ear and her breath whispering what I need to hear: *Love you.*

"Dan." Camille pulls my hands off her hips and laces her fingers into mine. "I want to tell you something."

Shit pops into my head. What did I do now? "I thought you wanted to move in." Maybe I don't have all my zombies in a row. Maybe—

"Dan!" Camille curls her arms around my neck and pulls my head down for a long, deep kiss. One hand strokes the back of my head. The other drops and smooths over my ass. Her mouth lingers on mine, touching, feeling, expressing.

And I stop wondering how I've screwed up again.

One last little kiss lands on my chin. "You worry *way* too much."

I'm grinning like a little kid. Like Bart when he wins a game. I don't need to worry anymore. "Maybe I need to burn off some energy." I nibble on her neck at the same time I brush my fingers over her breasts.

She tucks her head against my neck. "I see the same ability to read a situation in you that I see in your brothers." A new kiss lands on my chin. "Tom sees. Rob, I think, hears. And you..." A hug tightens around my waist. "I think you feel. Cold or hot. Tense or loose. It's in your body."

She must read that I'm not following by the look on my face. Camille laughs. "I haven't been with a lot of men. You're the fourth. But I will tell you this, gorgeous: I trust you infinitely more than I trusted any of them. With my life. With my *body*."

So she trusts me to get beyond the "almost." I like this idea.

She tugs on my hand. "Come with me."

Her bedroom is blander than I expected. Old furniture, dull colors. I barely register anything beyond the bed. I swing her up and drop her on her back at the same time I yank up her t-shirt. "Want," I growl.

"Hold on, mister pirate man." She pushes me off. "There are a couple of things we can do that will help me get where we want me to be." As she sits up, she leans over the side of the bed and pulls out a trunk.

Ah, yes, "the toys." This should be interesting.

"I think the reason I never got there with any other man is because I didn't trust them as much as I trust you." She flips open the lid. "What you do already is amazing and I think that with a little extra the sex is going to be—"

Inside the trunk I see a lot of long, black things. Things that cause pain.

I'm off her, kneeling on the edge of the bed. "You're into that? Why didn't you tell me?"

Camille's mouth rounds to a perfect circle. "I thought since you like playing that maybe we could try a few things."

Not this. "Not with what's in there." I point at the trunk. Not with things that hurt.

She looks at the toys, then up at me as she sits up. "Um, okay." She looks at the toys again, but I can see her disappointment. It's that same disappointment Lori showed when she was making her *Why didn't I wait and marry someone better?* face.

Like she thinks she's settling.

Camille frowns. "I've never had more than one orgasm at a time. Before you, everything was just a tickle, except when a guy used the toys."

She slams the trunk lid when I don't respond, but her face changes like she's had an idea. "Maybe the vibrator?"

I nod, but turn around. The light in the parking lot streams through her living room window and throws a pool of glare onto her couch. I walk out and drop into its center, blinking.

Shit, flits through my head again. I shouldn't freak out. She's not Lori. I don't even know what she's asking. But I know what I will and won't do.

But maybe I don't. Lori told me I was boring. She pointed her finger at my chest and said because I like to be on top and I like to kiss that I'm boring and I get what I deserve.

So I deserved her cheating on me. I deserved having to take that paternity test.

Camille sits on the couch but not close enough to touch. "Is this about—"

I know what she's going to say. "No." It's not. She might be spinning in my head but this isn't about her.

"Oh." She reaches to touch my arm but pulls back her fingers. "Was there someone else? Because I'm not into—"

"I've been with two women, okay? You and her."

Her frown works from her face to her shoulders and her chest. Camille slumps and sets her hands on her lap.

"That's how my life worked out. When Mom and Jeanie died, Dad gave up. Someone had to work. Tom and Rob needed me. So I tried to go to college and work full time but I couldn't handle it. I married Lori and I worked because I was at least good at being a firefighter."

Camille doesn't move. She doesn't ask questions, either. But the frown vanishes.

I rub my face. "The night of my injury, the police were already at the building when it blew. They'd been called on a domestic. Jason and I carried the mom and her two toddlers out. She'd been beaten pretty bad."

"Dan..." Her face takes on a completely different look and I wonder if maybe we can get through this.

But I'm not sure. "I've seen what violence does. So I won't hurt you, Camille. Even if you ask me to."

"That's not what it's about." She moves closer, but still doesn't touch.

I miss her fingers on my arm. I miss the closeness and the caring. And it's gone.

"We don't have to—"

I stand up. I need to pace. Move somehow. "I know stuff like this is a deal breaker. You're not going to want to stay with someone who's... boring. You shouldn't settle."

Camille stands, too. "Did I say that?" The frown reappears. "Why would I *ever* choose a box full of toys over *you*?"

For a moment, I'm silent. She might think that now, but women change their minds. They get bored. "I rather you told me now instead of a couple years into a marriage. I don't want to go through that again."

"That's not going to happen!" Camille twirls around. "Will you listen to me, please? You need to get beyond Lori. If you need to find someone to talk—"

"This is *not* about Lori!" I feel like punching the wall. But I won't.

"Some of it is. Obviously." Even my truncated ability to read women can see that she's angry. I see it in how she's standing.

"I will *not* hit you." Or tie her up. Or dominate her. "If it's a deal breaker I want to know *now*. Because I can't handle another six years of trying to heal."

"It's *not* a deal breaker! There are other things we can do." Camille's entire body slumps. "Can we talk about it? Please?"

I feel the zombies massing. They're familiar: Change this little bit of myself for a woman. Give up another area of my life so she's happy.

Sex with a woman I love makes *me* happy. Sex that's slow and genuine. And now pain wants to slither in.

"I'm going home." I need to think.

"Why?" I see tears. Her cheeks quiver. She's crying.

"I can't do pain anymore, Camille." I walk to the door.

"Dan!"

But I let the cheap door of her apartment close behind me.

I let it close off this part of my life.

I DROP MY KEYS AND MY PHONE ON THE KITCHEN COUNTER BEFORE I lock the door to the garage. I'm home. Alone.

Rob rounds the corner from the living room and stops in the open arch leading into the kitchen. "Where's Camille?"

I don't answer. I get two beers out of the fridge instead, and hand one to my annoying younger brother.

"What happened?" Rob flicks his cap onto the opposite counter, over the cabinet with the garbage can.

"We had a fight." I don't open my beer and it sits on the counter, mocking me.

Rob takes a pull at his. "What'd you do?"

"What did *I* do? Why is it always what *I* do?" Why do I always get what I deserve?

"Hey." Rob sets down his bottle and pats my back the way he pats Bart when he's upset. "Talk, brother."

What the hell am I supposed to say? It's not like he'd understand. That kind of shit doesn't bother him.

His sophomore year, he got into the kinky stuff for a while. Did a few things that raised my eyebrows. Sometimes I don't care if his high school years sucked. Sometimes I think he does shit like that to play it up and prove he's a "misunderstood bad boy."

He steps back. "She's got *toy* toys, doesn't she?"

My finger taps the counter, then the side of my beer, then the counter again, all on its own. Like it needs to be restrained. "*Fuck.*"

"It's not the end of the world." Rob rolls his eyes. "If she was into the lifestyle, she would have told you already. So they're exactly what she said they are—playthings."

I step away from the counter into the middle of the damned kitchen, where I can't touch anything. "I don't like it."

Rob rolls his eyes again. "Oh for God's sake! It's all the rage with the kids these days. It's like those damned vegan vampires of a couple of years ago—it's not nearly as potent as the real thing. It's sparkly spanking."

"I'm not doing that." I'm pacing. My body feels cold and I need to keep moving. "You know why."

Rob takes a long pull on his beer as he watches me walk two strides toward the dining area, then two strides back. "*Me* knowing why isn't important. You need to tell *her.*"

I stop. "I told her." Maybe I should open that beer. Bart's asleep. But it takes more than one beer to get a buzz going for me. I burn it off faster than it accumulates.

Except drinking never solved any problems.

"*All* the whys?" Rob doesn't get much of a buzz, either. So he's rational. Or at least as rational as my evil little brother can be.

"The ones that count."

He rolls his eyes again.

My phone buzzes. Rob's closer to it than me. He glances down as he takes another swig. "You should answer that."

I don't move. I need time to think. Hell, *she* needs time to think. If it's a deal breaker, then the deal needs to be broken.

Rob scoops up my phone and presses *accept* before I can stop him. "He's sorry and he's an overreacting idiot." His eyes narrow as he stares at me. "Right?"

I don't respond. How can I? I should be sorry. I'm screwing this up. But I can't do pain.

I can't.

Rob blinks and his eyebrows scrunch together. "Hey, listen Camille. He's home safe. We'll get it sorted."

Camille's indistinct voice pops from the phone, a flat, static-filled version of the woman I love. Because she's not here. She's far away.

I want to bang my head against the refrigerator until both it and door are well dented.

Rob says something else. Something about his flight out tomorrow. Then he hangs up. "You're thinking that if she likes the spanking and the tethers, she's lying if she tells you she will live without them." He sets his now empty bottle next to my phone. "Correct?"

I nod. Rob understands. "Lying to me and to herself."

Rob frowns. "Yes. As I have experienced."

"See? You know why." I'm pacing again. Why can't I hold still?

My brother grasps my shoulder. "Since when are my fucked-up girl-friends an example you should be looking to for dealing with your *not* fucked-up woman? Talk to Tom. Ask *Sammie*. Seriously. She's got a good head on her shoulders."

He's concerned. Actually, I believe, honestly concerned. I stand up straight. "I'm okay," I say. I shoulder the burdens of the world every day. How is this different?

"Anger isn't going to help, Dan."

Anger? "I'm not angry." Disappointed. Shocked. Maybe scared. But not angry. "I'll be angry if I get caught up in another lie."

He takes his hand off my shoulder. "I need to finish packing. You need sleep."

He flies out tomorrow morning at nine. "Be ready by six. I need to drop off Bart before taking you to the airport."

I won't have a moment to talk to Camille.

Rob nods and walks away, toward the guest bedroom, leaving me alone in my kitchen with my buzzing appliances and my buzzing life. Why don't I see this shit coming?

Why can't I read women better?

I turn off the lights and head to bed, knowing full well that I won't sleep tonight.

CHAPTER 18

Camille

I'm hoping Dan will at least talk to me this morning. I wasn't expecting what happened last night. At all. He's playful and I thought...

I stop pacing and sigh, pressing my fingers into my forehead. Most of the kids bounce and yell in their main rooms right now and my first pull-out starts in fifteen minutes.

Bart's not here. Again. Dan didn't call him in this morning, either.

I know he needs to take Rob to the airport but I think he's avoiding me.

The doors whoosh open. Bart skips in, his pack on his back, followed by Rob.

Not Dan. Rob.

Bart hugs my legs. "Are you coming home tonight?"

It takes all my effort to keep from sobbing right here in the Community Center lobby in front of the laughing front desk staff and my boyfriend's not-so-little younger brother.

I squat down to give Bart a hug. "I don't know."

Bart won't let go. "I miss you."

I was only gone this morning. I rub his shoulder as I watch his face. He looks genuinely upset.

I give him another hug. "Off to your room."

"Can I spend the whole day with you?" He hugs my legs again.

"We'll need to ask Ms. Cunningham."

Bart nods and runs off toward Sandy's room.

I watch him go. He picks up way more than a five-year-old should.

Next to me, Rob rubs the back of his head. He's not wearing a winter jacket—I don't think he brought one—and looks cold.

He stands with his feet planted too, his body angled like he has something to say. To my surprise, his phone stays in his pocket.

He watches Bart hang his pack in his cubby hook. "When we were kids, our father used to bring us up here at least once a week to the play area." He nods over to the large slide and ball pit that takes up a good chunk of space off the lobby.

"When Tom started middle school, after Mom and Jeanie died, Dan would bring us after school to play ball in the gym." He nodded to the other side of the building. "He took care of us."

"Dan told me how your mom passed. Said it was a car accident." Like Lori, he doesn't talk about it much.

Rob rubs his head again. "Tom and I are eighteen months apart." He shrugs. "Dan's six years older than Tom. Jeanie was in between." A smile flits across his face. "My sister and my oldest brother were almost exactly three years apart. Dan was in high school when the crash happened. Dad took it hard. Tom and I did not respond well to Dad's depression."

I'd been surprised when Dan told me their father wasn't flying in from Sedona for Bart's party. Or Tom's opening. "Is that why he's not around?"

Rob nods and leans closer. "I got Tom to promise to live-blog tomorrow night, mostly so I can share it with Dad."

Dan's bad boy brother doesn't seem all that naughty.

Quickly, I give him a hug. He blinks but quickly squeezes before stepping back.

"He told you what happened last night, didn't he?" I ask. "What should I do, Rob?" It pops out like so many other words have popped out over the last few days. Maybe all the Quidell men make me speak the truth, even if it's awkward.

He crosses his arms and watches Sandy's room, not me. "Dan had a good scholarship to a good college. He wanted to study structural engineering. Work big construction. Do you know why he became a firefighter?"

Because someone needed to work. "Your family needed the income."

"The crash happened two blocks from our house. Dan was the second person there." Rob's lips thin. "He saw the good first responders can do."

"I didn't know." Yet another bit of his life I didn't understand. "I figured he'd tell me when he was ready."

Rob nods toward the rooms. "He married Lori two weeks after they graduated."

Mary Beth is watching us from her room. I can't tell if she's frowning but I bet her eyes are narrow and her fists nice and tight.

Damn it, I think. *I don't need this right now*. And neither does Dan. We both need a little support. A little bit of compassion.

"I don't understand why he left last night." And why he refuses to talk to me. "Is he here, Rob? Will he come in? I can't go out. My class is about to start." I point at the door. Maybe I should go out anyway, the hell with my job.

"I think he feels boxed in." Rob's entire body shakes as if someone ran a finger up his spine. "Hell, Camille, I think he's *always* felt boxed in. Then you came along and let him out and he breathed for the first time in over a decade."

But Lori showing up and me bringing up something he thinks he'll need to accommodate because he *has* too, all produced the perfect storm of Dan worry. "Last night... reminded him of his box," I breathe. *Shit*.

The big clock over the Community Center door chimes. "I need to go." I squeeze Rob's arm and shuffle backward toward the rooms, even though I'm still confused. Still ready to sob. Still kicking myself for something that I think I should have seen coming.

But how could I have? Pain takes time to reveal. A man, even one as strong as Dan, can only handle so much at a time, no matter how much love and trust he feels. And Dan hadn't worked up to telling me what Rob just did.

I wave to Rob. "Tell him that when he's ready to talk, I very much want to talk."

"I will, Camille." Rob smiles as he, too, walks backward. He points and winks. "Think outside the box!"

Then he's gone, out the doors, on his way back to graduate school.

CHAPTER 19

Daniel

I feel numb this morning. Not angry. Not sad. Not depressed or frantic or anything else. Just numb. So I sent Rob into the Community Center with Bart instead of going in myself.

Thankfully, Rob avoided calling me names. Or accusing me of acting like a child. If I want to take a little time, I can take a little time.

I'm going to need to get over her sooner or later, anyway.

Bart didn't say much this morning. Though he did spend a lot of time hugging Uncle Robby and asking him when he'll be home again.

I rub my hand over my face and tap the fingers of my other hand on the steering wheel of my truck as I wait for Rob to come back out. He's been in there long enough already. I tap the steering wheel again.

Maybe he's talking some sense into Camille. The man knows how to sweet talk women. God knows it's gotten him in enough trouble over the past decade. The moment he decided girl cooties were something he *wanted*, no woman's been safe from his charms.

Rob has more than made up for my lack of field playing.

He's smiling when he saunters out the Community Center door

and I think my heart skips a beat and spikes right through the numbness.

Rob slams the door of my truck and the vehicle's entire frame rattles. He buckles in before picking up the coffee he made me go through the inconvenient and narrow drive-thru three blocks from the Community Center to get. The coffee smells like cinnamon and makes me hungry even though food is the last thing on my mind right now.

"I have fixed your problem." Rob pulls his phone out of his pocket and holds it up so I can see the screen. "Plane. Hour and a half. Security. Drive."

I start the truck. "What did you do?"

Rob shrugs. "Like I said, I fixed your problem." He swipes at his phone, ignoring me.

When we're on the freeway, halting and starting in morning traffic, I can't take the silence anymore. I need to know. "How?"

Rob shrugs again. "You know, you're acting the same way you acted when you had to haul your broken ass into the courtroom for the custody hearings. All 'man against the world' stoic hero. No tears shed. No emotion displayed. Because it gets in the way of your open can of whoop-ass."

"So? Bart's my priority. He needs stability." The brake lights of the car in front of us come on and I stomp a bit too hard. Rob slams against his seatbelt.

"Careful, bro. Got a test tomorrow. Don't need brain damage."

I glance at him. He sniffs at me as he takes a sip of his coffee. Quickly, he returns it to the cup holder before we hit another slowdown.

"What did you say to her?" A part of me wants to go all manic monster and rip shit down. Another part wants to crawl into bed and do whatever Camille wants so she won't leave.

I don't like either part.

"I gave her enough background I think she now understands your projection issues." He strokes his chin. "Or maybe you have a dissociation going on. I slept through Psych 101 so I don't know onto which page of the DSM of Mental Disorders you fall, my issue-filled brother."

"You aren't helping." More brake lights. More stomping.

Rob frowns and his coffee sloshes. "When she asks you to stop freaking the fuck out so the two of you can talk, you stop freaking the fuck out and sit down with her, okay?"

Of course I will. I owe it to her and to Bart to at least try. But I don't say anything more. I don't need Rob psychoanalyzing me.

Rob's phone, once again, appears. And, once again, his finger swipes.

I'd glare at him if I didn't need to watch the traffic. "Why don't you try living in the moment and not on your phone."

My little brother tucks away the device. He sips his coffee, his face stern the way mine is when I want Bart to listen. "What would I do 'in the moment,' Daniel?" This time, he slurps from his cup.

My hospital therapist's voice rings through my head: *See the world. Understand what's real and what's in your head.*

God damn it, my inner voices are ganging up on me and echoing my youngest brother.

I frown. Traffic picks up when we get around the curve and the sun's no longer in everyone's faces. I push my sunglasses up my nose. Rob returns to swiping at his phone.

At the airport, I pull up to the drop-off and put the truck in park. Traffic crawls by as other people look for a place to swing in. The ubiquitous airport information voice pipes from the speakers over the door, telling us all not to leave our bags unattended.

Rob unhooks his seatbelt. "Her name's Isolde, by the way."

"What?" Her name is Camille. He's not making sense—

The light dawns. Isolde must be his latest conquest. The one he didn't want to talk about when I picked him up. "What did you do this time, Robert?"

Absently, he taps his fingers on my truck's dash. "She's Mack's sister."

"You're fucking around with your roommate's sister?" I roll my eyes. "Is that why you're checking your phone all the time? To see if your roommate's kicked you out?"

The rawness of the pain on my little brother's face hits me hard in the gut. I almost reach for his arm, give his elbow a brotherly squeeze, but his look vanishes as fast as it appeared. "It's complicated." He points at me. "More complicated than your pathetic issues, dumbass."

"Of course." My little brother isn't a man who shies away from dating. Usually a new woman every week. "With you, it's always complicated."

The pain flits across his face again. "Unlike you, the life I've built lacks a solid reputation. My house, at least according to the female half of the human race, is not one of stability and emotional safety." Now Rob rolls his eyes.

We fall silent for a moment, both of us listening to the roar of the planes and the whoosh of the traffic. Two Quidell men, sitting by ourselves because it's the world against us.

Rob slaps his seat. "Time to go. Got a plane to catch."

I give him a quick back slap before he hops out. "Don't flunk your courses."

Rob walks to the back of the truck and pulls out his bag. When he comes around, he waves. "Don't spoil your son!"

My youngest brother strides through the sliding doors into the airport, his head low and his phone in his hand once again.

I pull out into traffic, also alone again, and head back to my life.

CHAPTER 20

Daniel

Through the speaker of my phone, I hear Tom's corporate desk chair squeak. I managed to catch him before he left his office for lunch. "Rob's right, you know."

"I don't know what to say to her." The parking lot of the fast food place I stopped at smells like old grease and engine oil. I glance at the burger in my hand, realizing it tastes the same, except with a coating of sugary red ketchup. I set it on the driver's seat, careful to keep it and all its toppings within the confines of its wrapper and the bag it sits on.

I'm outside so I can stretch my hamstring, even though it's too damned cold today. Winter better hurry up and go away.

"No, you don't." I hear Tom's keys jingle and his desk chair slide in. He's about to leave to meet Sammie. "If you did, you wouldn't be whining about it right now, would you? You'd take care of it like you always do."

I swing my shoulder. It's tightened up again, without Camille's touch to tame it. "You're more of an ass than Rob." Which I didn't think was possible.

Yet his words sound familiar. Then I remember: Rob said almost exactly the same thing. That I shoulder the burdens of the world.

Maybe I do. Maybe that's my role. But maybe my shoulders are full. Maybe I can't take shit sneaking up on me anymore. Maybe this one little thing that looks little to everyone else is just heavy enough I finally dropped to my knees. Which means my zombie list will catch up.

I scratch at my itchy stubble. How can I need help and fear the burdens help brings all at the same time? Because that's what this is. My fucking shoulders are full and I feel like the one person who might lift away some of the burdens is balancing on my forearm so she can reach. The weight's shifting, but I'm still carrying it. Now it's on my front instead of my back.

Or maybe I'm just being stupid and scared.

Not a great role model for my boy, that's for sure.

"I'm not ready to talk to her yet. Not out in the open like that, at the Community Center," I say into my phone. "I got shit in my own head to work out."

Tom snorts. "Yes, you do." He moves again and I hear muffled voices. "Sammie's here." I hear more talk. "She wants to know if you want us to pick up Bart tonight."

They'd do that? "What about the set-up at the gallery?"

I hear Sammie say something about not worrying.

"We're good. We're taking the day off tomorrow," Tom says.

I hear Sammie: "If you're anything like Tom, you'll have it all figured out by the time you see Camille at the gallery tomorrow night."

But I'm not like Tom. My brother isn't selfish. He's the one who sacrificed to move in with me after my injury because I needed the help.

"Listen," Tom says. "We'll meet you at your place around dinner time. You need us, just text. I mean it." My brother says good-bye and cuts the call.

I set my phone next to the chewy, now-cold burger. It sits on my seat, wrapped up so it doesn't stain my upholstery. Standing in the cold, my foot on the truck's running board as I un-cinch my leg muscles, I close my eyes, counting the way I'm supposed to, when the world gets out of control. Taking that deep breath to calm my body because, as the docs said, the first step to regaining your strength is to silence the nag-zombies in your head.

What if it's too late? What if...

I rub my face again. What if, when I'm ready to talk to her, she doesn't want to talk to me ever again?

Shit.

Am I moving too fast again? Too slow? What if she feels like *she's* settling?

I see zombies everywhere. Or maybe Bart's sharks. But I know I'm not one of his superheroes.

Or the pirate Camille wants.

Or, right at this moment, the good independent contractor my contacts want. I rub my leg again. God knows being a good firefighter again is out of the question.

Father. Lover. I thought, too, if my luck held, maybe a husband again.

I don't know who I am. I throw the burger and the equally cold fries in the trash and drop my ass in front of my steering wheel.

Or what I should be.

CHAPTER 21

Camille

I wrap my hair into a loose French knot and pin it up, carefully leaving tendrils around my face. Smoky eye makeup follows. My shimmering ocean green shawl covers my shoulders and I wear a dark blue long sleeved dress and nice boots, because it's darned cold tonight.

It's time for Tom's gallery opening.

Tom said to give Dan his space when he and Sammy picked up Bart yesterday, so I've let him have his space. Dan didn't bring him in this morning. His call to the Center said something about helping Tom and Sammie finish their gallery set-up.

So I didn't text Dan. Or call, even though I *know* set-up is done.

I know because Sammie volunteered Monday evening to help me "think outside the box." I figured if anyone could help, it would be Dan's brother's communications-genius fiancé.

At first, I was embarrassed asking her for sex tips. But it turns out that Sammie knows a thing or two. We spent a good two hours discussing our big, beautiful men and I'm sure Tom had a wonderful night because if it.

Tempted as I was to give myself a little relief, I'm wrapping my horniness up in my nice dress and boots, just for Dan.

The drive to the gallery takes longer than I thought it would, with the ice. I concentrate on the road, welcoming it as a distraction from Dan as much as cursing it for making my little car skid around corners. When I see Dan's gigantic red truck, I maneuver into the tight space in front of it, thinking about the tight spaces I can get into with Dan.

Tight spaces made accessible by all the oil I'm going to massage into his skin.

A tap on my window startles me so much I gasp, and it pulls me from my revelry. Sammie stands in the street in a beautiful indigo dress with what looks like Tom's coat over her shoulders.

I roll down my window. "What are you doing out here? Get back inside before you freeze to death."

"You're here!" Sammie bounces on her high heels. "They're inside. Bart's drawing pictures for the guests and Tom has Dan walking around the gallery with his phone on video chat so Rob can see." She smiles. "I think everyone at his school is watching. Don't tell Tom. He's nervous enough as it is."

I somehow suspect it's not just Rob's classmates who are watching.

"I have something I want to show you before we go in." She's grinning like the world's all rainbows and kittens.

"Okay." I really just want to go in and find Dan, but Sammie's excitement is contagious.

"Won't take long. I promise." She grips my arm after I shut my door so neither of us slips on the icy sidewalk.

I nod. We help each other over the snow on the curb. Sammie rubs her hands together and stomps her feet.

"We need to go inside before you turn into an indigo popsicle." I tug on her arm. We can have our girl talk where it's warm.

"This way." Sammie's grin returns and she pulls me down the street. "I need your opinion before I show Tom." She stops at a door and pulls a key out of her clutch. "I think it's perfect, but I want to know what you think first, as another artist."

Inside, we climb the stairs to the upper level. It's a wide open and spacious space, with huge windows facing the skyline. Some old furniture sits in a corner and I think the loft must have been an office at one time.

"It's gorgeous," I say. "Beautiful view. I bet it has incredible light during the day."

Sammie twirls around. "I think he's going to like it."

I haven't known Tom long enough to know for sure, but I think so. *I'd* like it. "If he doesn't, I'll move in with you."

Light from the signs outside, on the street, flood the loft. Sammie stands in the middle of a puddle of red and blue, watching me the way I watch my students.

Her relationship with Tom took a very different course from mine and Dan's. Like with a lot of his painting's subjects, Tom immediately saw in Sammie what she needed illuminated.

I wish I'd seen what I needed to see with Dan a lot earlier. None of this would have happened.

Sammie pats my arm. "Tom's told me how rough Dan's injury and divorce were on him. On the whole family, really."

She waves and I take the stairs first. Her heels click as we walk toward the door. "I think Dan feels he needs to keep the world in order, or everything will fall apart."

"You're right." He does. "But I need to know *he's* not going to fall apart."

Sammie squeezes my hand. "You know, when I met Tom, I didn't think I deserved someone as good as him. He opened up the path I needed to walk in order to see that I do."

I don't know if she's referring to me or to Dan. Right now, the path is flooded and the cold water is freezing my feet.

And Dan's, too.

"He deserves so much more than he's allowing himself," I say. Dan's good at his work. He's brilliant with his son. And he's always there for his family.

Sammie takes my hand and pulls me down the street, toward the gallery. "Did you know you're the only person he talks about? Not his contracts or how well his business is doing. It never dawned on him to ask for logo design help because for the last six months, whenever Tom and I visit and it's Ms. Frasier this, Ms. Frasier that. How happy Bart is. How wonderful you are to both of them. He's been in love with you for a lot longer than you think."

We stop just outside the gallery door. Light pours through the wide plate glass front window, around the stylish, bold lettering of the gallery name. Inside, a crowd mills about, with knots of people gathering in front of several large, colorful paintings, all of Sammie.

I don't know what to say. I feel my chest tighten and a new hiccup force its way into the back of my throat.

"Hey, hey." Sammie takes my hands again. "Do you want me to send him out? My friend Andy and I will watch Bart if you want to take him down the street. Get coffee."

I shake my head. "It's Tom's special night. Both Dan and Bart want to be here." I give her a hug. "I do, too."

Sammie opens the door and a sweet chiming fills the gallery entrance. "We better go in before the boys miss us."

I nod, following her inside.

۞

DAN'S EYES GROW BIG WHEN HE SEES ME. "YOU CAME?" HE LOOKS around before holding up his phone. "Rob wants to say hi."

On the screen, Rob waves. A cute blonde woman leans in and waves too.

"Hi, Rob," I say.

He gives me the thumbs up.

"Hold on." Dan and Rob chat for a moment, then Dan slips the phone into his pocket. "Seems his friend wants to get ice cream."

I want to push him into the corner and poke my finger into his chest all while yelling "What the *fuck* do you think you're doing, mister!" Then rip off his suit so he lets loose all his pent-up anger and frustration with hard thrusts and breath-stealing kisses.

But that's not going to happen.

"Do you want me to take your coat? There's a place set aside in the back." He points to a dark hallway leading away from the little corner set up for Bart.

Behind Dan, in a small, cordoned off area, a handsome dark haired man sits at a low table next to Bart, coloring in a picture of a puppy. The cubby is separated from Sammie's nudes, and contains several drawings of Bart and his action figures, plus a couple done by the little master himself, including two he did in class, for me.

I pull off my coat and hand it over. "Thanks."

Dan's face takes on an impressive expression of awe as I adjust my dress and shawl. I realize this is the first time he's seen me in non-work make-up and clothes. And most likely the first time in a dress.

"You look stunning." He reaches out to touch my hand but stops. Then his fingers vanish under the folds of my coat.

His suit's nice, cut well, and I wonder if it originally started as court attire. My poor boyfriend looks quite uncomfortable. "You look every inch the handsome man you are, Dan Quidell."

I'm going to do something about this.

"I'll drop your coat." Dan walks backward for a few steps, watching me. "Are you staying?"

"Yes."

He looks impassive. And maybe a little afraid. "So we can talk?"

He wants to talk. Finally. "Yes."

When he walks by the table, he whistles to Bart and points.

"Hey, little man!" I kneel with my arms wide open, waiting for Bart to notice me.

"Ms. Frasier is here!" Bart all but leaps into my arms and hugs me with all his five-year-old strength.

The man at the table stands and offers his hand. "I'm Andy, Sammie's friend. You must be Camille."

"Yes." We shake. "Nice to meet you."

Bart tugs on my hand and I lean down. "Mr. Andy's not a good drawer but don't tell him because he's nice and he will be sad."

Andy swallows a guffaw. "From the mouths of babes."

Bart leans against my hip. "Are you coming home tonight? I miss you."

"I miss you, too." More than I realized.

He clutches my legs. "I want you to come home."

"I'm here now." I hoist him up but the strain hurts my back. The slight heel on my boots aren't helping. "I can't carry you for long, okay? You're too big."

Bart wiggles. "It's okay." He hugs me again and pats my shoulder as if he's the teacher and I'm the student. "I can walk."

I set him down. "You *are* a big boy and I'm very proud of you for behaving so well, and for showing your pictures alongside your uncle's."

Bart stands proud as he sticks out his thumb the way he does when he's painting. "Look!" He pulls me to one of the display walls.

One of Tom's pencils of Dan and Bart catches my eye first. Both father and son lounge in a kiddie pool, in Dan's backyard. Both dressed as superheroes, splashing away. Dan's long sleeved shirt sticks to his sculpted torso, but Tom hinted at the scars underneath. The edges of the drawing give a sense of the terrible world beyond the pool, but the world need not fear. Doctor Bartman and Minion One will save the day.

Right next to the pencil is one of Bart's drawings. One I've never seen before. It's his dad, and him. And me.

And we're happy.

"I made that one for you." Bart points. "I want you to come home."

The hiccup makes it past my lips. I cover my lips with one hand and hug Bart close with the other.

All my thoughts of seducing Dan vanish. He needs love tonight more than he needs sex, no matter how much I want him to know how horny he makes me.

Andy takes Bart's hand. He nods toward the hallway. "Dan's taking his time back there. Why don't you go check on him? Doctor Bartman and I have this under control, don't we, buddy?"

Bart nods. "I'll draw you a new picture."

When Bart tugs on Andy's hand, Sammie's friend winks. I stifle a frown. Does everyone know? But at least they're looking out for us.

I run my hands down the front of my dress. Time for a talk.

I tiptoe down the hallway as best I can in my boots. Shadows slide across the bare-brick walls, cast by a lone light I suspect is coming from the coat room.

The sounds of the gallery diminish the deeper I go, as much, I suspect, from my own awareness of my heartbeat as from the walls' muffling. My heels click. My dress rustles. My body remembers how good Dan feels against my skin. And how warm and alive his cock tastes in my mouth.

I stop and close my eyes for a second. I need to get my horniness in check. Dan's my priority.

I hear Dan brush against the doorframe ahead of me. The light goes out. He's about to come out of the coat room.

When I step in front of him, he shivers, surprised. "Camille."

Quickly, I splay my fingers over his chest. He looks delicious in his suit. I give him a shove backward. "We have a moment. I'd like to take advantage of it."

Dan frowns but slides his feet back into the coat room. It's dark and I can't make out anything but a couple of piles of jackets, a desk, and a high counter against the back wall. Artwork covers all surfaces, but I can't make out colors. And it smells like donuts.

My mouth waters.

"I don't know if this is—" Dan stops talking when I curl my arms around his neck.

"When I said that I would *never* choose a box of toys over you, I meant it." I press my entire body against his.

"Maybe now. But what happens in six months? A year? When the new wears off and you want more." He's arguing but he's not stepping back. His hands drop to my waist and his fingers grip my hips.

"What about you, huh? In six months when the new wears off, are you going to start noticing how other women look at you? Because they do. Are you going to wonder about what you've missed?" It's not Dan's personality to play the field, but I need to make a point.

It's not *my* personality to push him away.

His frown deepens. "*No.* Why would I do that? I'm not an idiot."

"Then why would you think *I* would? Learning how to make love with you is an opportunity. A wonderful, brilliant opportunity I won't pass up."

CHAPTER 22

Daniel

Camille's scent fills my senses. It's ylang ylang. Like the candles. Like the night I said *the woman I love*.

She's right here, pressed against me and more gorgeous than I thought possible.

And she wants me. I rub my thumb over her hip. I don't feel lace under the clingy fabric of her dress, but I do feel it when I rub my palm over the top of her thigh.

Stockings. And no panties.

"An opportunity?" I ask.

"To learn. To build something special that's only between us." She gently kisses my chin.

"But—"

Camille lays a finger on my lips. "I worry too, Dan. I worry about what your family thinks of me. I worry about my job and I worry about not making enough money. I worry about Bart because I know it's going to be difficult to get him interested in math. And I worry about you working too hard. And about you worrying too much."

My body tightens on its own. My arms wrap around her waist. My shoulders drop down. And I bury my face against her neck. "I'm sorry," I whisper.

Camille moves us a step to the side. She leans against the counter along the back wall and I hoist her up, setting her bottom on the smooth surface.

My back straightens. She's high enough I no longer need to stoop. I can stand tall.

She kisses my cheeks, my chin, my lips. "This isn't about the toys, or settling in our relationship, or, I think, the stress of your current life."

I don't know what to say. She's right. It isn't. I have an inkling about a deeper problem, but I don't know what it is. Like Tom told me, if I did, I would have taken care of it a long time ago.

"I want to be with you, Daniel Quidell. I'm not giving you up without a fight." Her kiss is strong and warm. Loving.

I bury my face in her neck again. "I'm sorry." It's the only thing I can say.

"You can talk to me." She kisses my temple again. "You could talk to a therapist if you want. Someone who's on the outside. It's up to you."

What is happening here? How did I get to this place? I'm stuck in the slush of my life and I think Camille might be offering me a lifeline.

All I want is to let her warm my cold bones.

"I want you to know that Sammie and I had a talk last night. We discussed our Quidell men." Her fingers stroke my neck and my arms.

I chuckle as I imagine them comparing notes. "Now I have to worry about living up to Tom." The suggestive tone in her voice distracts me from my internal whining.

Or maybe I just don't want to think about it anymore.

She leans in. "We talked because I want you to enjoy sex with me as much as I enjoy it with you." One hand works into my hair. The other roams over my crotch. "I think you will like what I learned."

My cock is suddenly very much alive. And very much not worrying about the world anymore. "Right now? Here? Someone might come in."

Camille leans back. Her body quickly disengages from mine, and cool air fills the void between us. I frown.

She touches my cheek. "I love you, Dan. I trust you. I *want* you. I don't think you accept how insanely sexy and wonderful you are. I want to show you. Prove it to your skeptical mind. But I do need one thing before we move forward."

A good pounding? I think.

I must have smirked because she kisses the bridge of my nose. But she's not smiling.

Shit, flits through my head. What else could there be? "What?"

"I need to know that you want to deal with the worrying." She looks at me with her teacher face, gauging my reactions.

"I *am* dealing with the worrying." Every goddamned moment of my life I deal with the worrying.

"Dan." Her kiss is intense. But the desire I feel isn't the desire I was expecting. Her body tenses. Her brow pulls together. "Please. It's like you're keeping your soul in a box under the bed."

I'm not horny anymore. I'm confused.

"At the zoo, you put a lot of effort into keeping me. You put insane amounts of effort into your business and your family. Promise me you'll put the same determination into *yourself*."

I hear a couple of people shuffling down the hall. The owner must be bringing patrons back to pick up their coats.

Quickly, I lift Camille off the counter and set her next to me. She smooths her dress and runs her fingers over her hair. "Where's the light switch?" she calls. "It's dark in here."

I grasp her hand before I realize what I'm doing. When the light flicks on, we're staggering toward the door. "On our way out."

I smile my best smile and we push by, all but running down the hallway.

Before we round the corner, Camille tugs on my hand. We stop, standing together in the dim light, my family in front of us and the intrusions of the world behind.

"Please think about what I said. Maybe we can talk again later this week?"

She's not coming home with me. Though I don't know why she would.

I hoped that she would always have my back, no matter how stupid I act or how much pressure being with her adds to my burdens.

But her eyes don't say *adding*. Her eyes say *subtracting*.

Maybe she has my back in ways I don't understand.

The light in the coat room goes off again. "We need to go." I tug on her hand.

Together, we walk into the gallery.

And I need to find a way to make that *together* as real as the concern I see in her eyes. Because at this point, I know that burden's completely mine.

❧

I WATCH CAMILLE PULL AWAY. HER HATCHBACK SPUTTERS AND IT takes a significant amount of effort for me not to call her back. But she's right—I need to think. My need for her pulls at my gut and, deep inside, it's not all that different than when I lost Mom and Jeanie. But I think that's part of the problem.

I glance at the gallery when I hear the sing-songy chime go off because someone swung open the door. Sammie glides out into the cold, laughing, her shoulders bare, Tom right after her. They hurry down the sidewalk hand in hand without noticing me. I watch them go. Tom curls his arm around his fiancé, protective of her skin.

She laughs again.

I walk back to the truck. Bart's leaning his head against the seat, half asleep and bundled up in his winter coat and hat. He only stirs a little when I open the door. Outside, Tom and Sammie stop at another door, their heads close together.

Even from this distance, I see how Tom watches her. It shows in his paintings, too. Tom always sees the essence of a situation. And the essence of people.

Bart stirs. "I'm cold." But he closes his eyes again and returns to leaning his head against the seat.

"Sorry, buddy." I start the truck, flicking on the heater, and watch

Tom and Sammie enter the other building. They close the door behind them just as a blast of still-chilly air washes over Bart and me.

No heat until the engine warms up. The engine has to do what the engine has to do before the fire can take hold.

I pull the truck out onto the street and head home, my to-do list popping into my mind as I drive, the same as it always does. What's left to get Bart ready for school tomorrow? Am I prepared for my meetings next week? Do I need to shovel the walk again?

Just like an engine, I don't seem capable of changing, unlike my artist brother. Out on the freeway, I remember Rob asking me what Tom's secret was. How he solidified his relationship with Sammie so quickly.

My brother Tom reads the moment, not the demands laid on him. He sees what needs seeing, not checklists. Or threats of terrible futures.

Is that what Camille meant about putting effort into myself? Does she think I don't keep myself safe?

Or maybe *too* safe.

I wish I knew.

But tonight made me sure of one thing: I need Camille in my life.

And if that means I need to push through things that make me upset, then I'm going to take a chance, even if the shit might hit the fan.

I'm going to do what she needs me to do.

CHAPTER 23

Camille

The morning after Tom's gallery opening, Bart runs in, hugs my leg, and bounces into Sandy's room. I half expect Dan to do the same thing but he stops in front of me in his wrinkled button-down and chinos.

"You look happier." He's happy like he's come to a conclusion. My heart thumps. "Do you feel better?" I want to jump into his arms. Give him a big kiss right here, in front of all the other teachers.

Dan clasps his hands behind his back but doesn't stand like a college professor, the way Rob does. He squares his shoulders and pirate smirks where he stands in the bright sunlight spilling from the skylights, not saying anything.

My heart skips a beat. "Dan, don't keep secrets." What is he up to? His hair is messier than usual today, and I don't think he shaved.

My heart skips a beat again and I feel like bouncing, too.

He shakes his head and holds a finger to his lips. His foot slides back. He's walking away. "I'm working too hard." But he winks.

"Dan!" The clock chimes and I look over my shoulder. When I look back, he's waving as he dashes through the door.

Damn it. I almost text Sammie. Maybe I should text her. See if Dan said anything to Tom. Or maybe I should text Tom.

Sandy walks up, watching the door more than me. "Class time," she says. "Got everything worked out with Dan?" She nods toward the door.

"How did you know we were having issues?" It's not like I talk to my coworkers about my relationship. They're not exactly supportive.

Sandy chuckles. "All the kids keep asking me why Ms. Frasier is mopey. And Bart's been sad. Acting out in my room, though I suspect he's been extra good for you, hasn't he?"

I didn't know. "Why didn't you say something? I could have talked to him." He's usually such a good kid. "What's he been doing?"

Sandy shrugs. "Normal mad child behaviors. Not doing what he's asked to do. Taking toys from the other kids." She nods at the door. "Frowning a lot, like you and his daddy."

No matter how hard I tried, my Dan problem spilled over into work.

Sandy pats my arm. "Let's go. The little ones await."

I follow her back to the rooms, listening to the volume and pitch of the kids as they play, in case there's a problem. Or if someone needs a hug.

I glance over my shoulder again, hoping, maybe, Dan will come running back in, because I think a hug right now is what we both need.

DURING THE THREE O'CLOCK SNACK BREAK, ALL MY KIDS RETURN TO their main rooms, Bart included. On Fridays the teachers always do a theme—today is spring rain showers—and I painted rainbows on everyone's cheeks. They're all excited to show off their colors. I walk them down the hall, the six little artists who spend their time after lunch with me, dropping them off one by one with their teachers and their aides.

Bart's the last to drop off. He holds my hand, skipping along next to me, a rainbow on each of his cheeks. "When will the snow melt?" he asks.

He's been asking all sorts of weather-related questions today. When will it rain? Can I build a mudman the way I build a snowman? Why can't you touch rainbows? Why do you plant flowers? My daddy doesn't plant *anything* and there are flowers all over my yard.

"The flowers are yellow!" Bart says. "Some are purple. I like the purple ones the best." He skips along. "Will you come for pizza tonight?"

At Sandy's door, he hugs my waist. "Daddy misses you too."

Sandy appears in the door before I can answer Bart's question. Grinning, she leans down to Bart. "Your uncle is here."

I look down the hall and into the atrium. "Dan's not picking up Bart today?" I was going to make him stay and talk.

Tom and Sammie sit at one of the far tables, behind a planter, out of sight of my room. They're dressed for work, both in their corporate attire, as if they'd just come from the office. When they see me notice them, they both get up, waving.

"Uncle Tommy!" Bart jumps up and down. "Auntie Sammie!"

When they're close enough, Bart looks up at Sandy for permission to run to his uncle.

"Go on," she says.

Bart takes off, leaping for his uncle like a little superhero. Sandy pats my arm. "No more pull outs today. You go on, too."

"What?" She's telling me to leave early?

Sammie pulls an envelope out of her purse as they get close. Sandy winks and backs away, into her room.

"You all packed for your big weekend, buddy?" Tom glides Bart through the air and Bart stretches out, arms straight in front, legs back, laughing.

"Hey, Minion Two-Two, concrete floor." I point at the ground.

Tom frowns and spins Bart up onto his hip. "Ms. Frasier's a buzzkill, Doctor Bartman."

Bart screeches when Tom tickles his belly.

I glance at Sammie. "Weekend? It's Wednesday."

She smiles. "We're taking the rest of the week off and Doctor Bartman's staying with us, isn't that right, buddy?"

Bart screeches again. "Can we go to the zoo?"

Sammie pats his back. "Of course we can." She hands over the envelope. "We're supposed to give you this."

I take it. Across the front, in Dan's blocky and masculine hand, is "To m'lady, Ms. Frasier."

Bart points at the door. "Did you bring Mr. Pickles?"

Tom chuckles. "The kitty is at home, buddy."

Bart frowns. "Oh. Did you bring juice boxes?"

Now Sammie chuckles. "We'll have him home before bedtime Sunday."

They're taking him through the weekend?

Tom puts Bart down. "Go get your stuff." He shoos Bart toward Sandy's room. "And don't distract the other kids, Doctor Bartman. You're incognito, remember?"

Bart puts his finger to his lips and makes a shushing sound before tiptoeing into the room.

I watch him go. "He knows what 'incognito' means?"

Tom shrugs. "Of course he does. He's a superhero." He walks by, toward Sandy's door, following Bart.

Sammie leans close. "Dan called Tom this morning. Said the two of you needed time alone." A knowing smile brightens her face. "I want *all* the details. Every single one." Her hug surprises me, but only a little. "Time to see Mr. Pickles, Doctor Bartman!" She winks and helps Bart zip his jacket when he reappears.

Tom waits, Bart's bag in his big hand. "Dan is still confused, Camille. But he's trying." They walk out the door together, Bart between Tom and Sammie, on the way to a kid-filled weekend.

My fingers jitter when I look down at the envelope in my hand. What's Dan doing? My stomach's flip-flopping because...

Because I'm happy. He's trying and it makes me happy.

I open the envelope.

Inside, on a white index card, are three words: "Meet me outside." That's it. Just "Meet me outside."

I run for the door, not returning to my room to fetch my purse. Not to clean up. Not even to get my coat.

Because Dan's here. And he's waiting.

CHAPTER 24

Camille

The cold hits me hard when I run through the door. It's warmer today, but my breath still steams in the air. The sun shines, but a breeze kicks up the nippiness.

I don't care. Dan's here, somewhere.

Sammie waves as she closes the passenger door of Tom's big red truck. Bart's in his booster, tucked into the corner seat behind her. Their truck rumbles to life and Tom pulls out of the lot.

I don't see Dan's truck. It's the newer model of Tom's and just as big. And just as red. Both trucks stand out. It's not like Dan could hide it. I look around again. Am I on the wrong side of the building?

I stomp my feet, wondering if I should get my jacket. Where's Dan?

Not far from the Community Center entrance where I stand, the driver's side door of a big, shiny, silver car swings open. It's one of those sleek, fast German sedans, the expensive ones.

Dan's head appears over the top of the door and he leans against the car's frame. With one gloved hand, he points at the car's passenger side. "Are you going to get in?"

The car stands at attention and guarding its parking space like a good dog. Or a cheetah.

"Where's your truck?"

Dan grins as he saunters up the steps, leaving the car wide open. "At home."

"Did you buy that thing?" I point at the car.

"Rental. For the week." He curls his arm around me and I immediately warm. Even through his jacket, he gives off enough heat to stop any hypothermia creeping into my bones. "A gorgeous woman deserves a gorgeous ride."

"Dan!" I shiver as he unzips his jacket and pulls me inside. Damn, the man is warm. And hard. And my head fits perfectly against his neck when I wrap my arms around his chest.

"Will you forgive me for being an idiot?" He nuzzles the top of my head.

"You're not an idiot. You're overworked and you've had too much shit go wrong in your life and you just need to learn ways to deal with it that won't drive me insane."

Dan glances around. He watches a middle-aged woman in workout clothes walk by before saying anything. "You know, when you put it that way, it makes sense."

I poke his chest. "I don't always know what to say! My therapy expertise is in art."

"You're damned good at the physical, too." Dan watches a mom pushing a stroller walk by. "In the car." He nods toward the sedan. "Please."

I step around his big body and walk down the steps to the car's passenger side door, doing as he asks. It glides open like it floats on fairy dust. "Your car is distracting."

Dan chuckles and twists his big frame into the driver's seat. He barely fits. "No to-do list for the week, though I did make several reservations."

The car all but swallows me whole when I get in. It doesn't smell at all. Not even a whiff of cleaner. It's like the Germans managed to engineer a bright spring day into the ventilation. And I've never in my life sat in a seat with such perfect lumbar support. I buckle in and lean my head against the buttery leather.

Dan starts up the car. It purrs to life, the dash lighting up and all the indicators pinging their welcome. Even its flickers and chimes scream luxury.

"You went all out, didn't you?"

He doesn't take it out of park. He does, though, start the heater. "Got a hot date with a hot woman. Doing my best to impress. Because, starting today, I'm going to work less. Relax more. And try new things."

Dan shifts as best he can in the seat, to angle his body toward mine. "It's time to stop fearing the worst. So I thought we could go back to your apartment for a while."

I see his chest tighten.

My reaction blurts out uncensored. "We will not!" I slap the dash. "You don't *want* to! It's obvious in your shoulders that you don't want to! We will *not* dive right into something that makes you uncomfortable."

"But…"

"How is setting aside a belief that is obviously important to you because you think I will leave, *not* you settling?" Why can't he see what he's doing?

Dan blinks and his cheeks tighten. "Then tell me what I am supposed—" Dan flings open his door.

"What?" But I see her. Lori stalks toward the car from the same rented sedan she had the night of Bart's birthday party.

"Stay in the car, Camille." Dan slams his door.

I think several unteacher-like words. Lori would show up now, wouldn't she? Ruin what otherwise is turning out to be a spectacular day.

Not this time. I get out, slam the passenger door and walk around the car, standing between her and Dan. I'm cold again, but I don't care. She's not going to cause Dan's already too high stress level to shoot through the roof or take up our entire weekend making us file police reports.

"The Community Center daycare has the right to restrict access to the grounds of any non-custodial parent. You are not to enter the building or the parking lot. Get back in your car and leave." I'm between her and Dan before she gets half way across the lot.

Lori Taylor-Quidell glares over my shoulder, at Dan. "Since when can you afford a car like that?" she yells. "Did you hide something during the settlement? Tell me the truth, you pathetic worthless little man!"

"*Little?*" She's crazier than I thought. I hold up my hand. "Don't talk to her, Dan. Don't—"

"Why are you here, Lori?" Dan slaps the top of his rented German sedan. "Because you don't give a shit about your son. You never have."

Lori pokes at the air like she's trying to blind Dan with the tip of her finger. "I want what's mine!"

"You got yours when the judge sent you packing!" Dan flips her off.

"Oh, really? I put up with the whiny Quidell boys for *seven years*! Tom's the only one of you to grow a pair after your mother died! Living with you and all your tight-assed workaholic moping damaged me!"

I open and close my mouth, stunned silent. "Did she just say that?"

Anger reddens Dan's neck. "I swear she wasn't this crazy when we were married."

Lori thrusts her fists into her waist in very much the same way as Bart does when he's upset. "You owe me! And now you're driving around in a car like *that*?"

"You checking up on me?" Dan walks around me but stops several feet from Lori.

Around us, several people stop to watch. A few others continue into the Center.

Now Dan points at Lori. "*Owe* you? I worked my fingers to the bone for you! I stuffed my life into a box because I needed your help with my brothers and I was too damned immature to realize..."

Dan pivots. He turns around completely where he stands on the asphalt, his face a mask of shock. "...what it was doing to me. When my injury happened the box got smaller and I couldn't breathe anymore. Which is why I freaked out the first time the person I love— the person who loves and wants to help *me*—said something I thought would make my box that much tighter."

I'm in his arms before he stops speaking.

"I didn't hear what you said. I heard what I feared." Dan folds his jacket around me. "I'm sorry I didn't trust you, Camille."

"I've always trusted you," I whisper. "I trusted you'd figure this out."

Dan stiffens. He's not looking at me. He's looking at the Community Center entrance.

"I didn't do anything!" Lori screeches.

I look over my shoulder. The Community Center is two blocks from the city's police station and main fire house. We get uniformed officers coming in and out all day, usually stopping to pick up a cup of coffee. Sometimes they stay and play ball with the kids. We also usually have one or two off duty, out-of-uniform officers on the grounds most afternoons, in the Center's workout facilities.

Like today.

Mary Beth, the other teacher who's been giving me dirty looks since the strawberry picking field trip, stands on the step, shivering. Behind her, Sandy opens the entrance door. Mary Beth points at Lori as our uniformed officer strides through, his eyes on Lori and only Lori.

Another officer walks out into the cold—the woman named McMillian who took our statements the first time Lori showed up— and pats her face with the corner of her t-shirt. She must have been in the gym.

The uniformed officer walks by, nodding once. "You!" He points at Lori. "State your name."

"Why?" Lori backs away.

Up on the step, Mary Beth calls out. "Her name is Lori Taylor-Quidell."

The officer looks at Dan, who nods.

The officer continues walking toward Dan's ex. "The on-duty teachers and the staff of the Community Center have informed me that, by court order, you are not allowed on the premises."

"We want to file a complaint!" Mary Beth calls. When she looks at me, her expression says it all: *I'm sorry.*

"You need to come with me." The uniformed officer pulls out his cuffs.

"But... but..." Lori holds perfectly still when the officer takes her arm.

Dan's big chest presses against my back, blocking the cold. "An arrest will get her to leave us alone," he whispers. "The first time she disappeared was right after the judge ordered her to put in effort to see Bart."

I look up. His gaze moves from watching the officer haul away Lori to the other teachers on the steps, and back again.

I turn in his arms. His lists are surfacing again, even if he's finally broken out of his box. I feel them in the tightness of his lower back and see them in the sadness around his eyes. He thinks he's going to have to take care of Lori's intrusion. Be there for all the report filings. Make sure Tom and Sammie know. I'm pretty sure he thinks his life just killed all the joy he'd hoped to generate this weekend, with me.

"Hey." I kiss his jaw. "Look at me."

Dan blinks, but smiles when he looks down into my eyes.

"I'll get my coat. And I'll be right back. Okay?"

He kisses my forehead before he nods. His arms release and my wonderful boyfriend takes a step back.

I run up the steps to Sandy and McMillian. Stomping my feet, I rub my arms. "Do you need us? I mean really, truly need us here?"

McMillian looks over my shoulder at Dan. Her cheeks are red and she steps side-to-side the way someone who just stopped a run does. "Big plans?"

"Dan needs a break." A real break. One from the weight of his life. "She can't ruin the weekend for him." For *us*.

Sandy pulls her sweater tight around her middle. She catches Mary Beth's gaze and for a second, it looks as if the other two teachers are communicating telepathically. "He does need a break. So do you." She nods toward me. "He worries too much and you shoulder too much of the world."

I snort. It's not pretty, but it's how my body reacts. "*I* shoulder too much of the world?"

Sandy rolls her eyes and pats my arm.

I return my attention to McMillian, hoping maybe I have a little of that teacher telepathy, as well. All I can think is *please please please let us go. Please.* World shouldering or not, Lori can't ruin this moment for Dan. Or me.

In the lot, Lori yells something at the officer.

"Oh, resisting arrest." McMillian sniffs. "Not smart."

Mary Beth shakes her head when Lori pulls her wrists away from the officer. "We'll file the complaint."

"You two will need to file witness reports on Monday." But McMillian's grin tells me all I need to know.

"Thank you!" I'd hug her but she's a cop.

She smiles though, and gives Dan a thumbs-up.

And I run for my coat and purse.

DAN'S HUMMING. HIS FACE IS BURIED IN MY CLEAVAGE AND HE'S humming like a happy little kid.

Somehow, he managed to find a secluded spot surrounded by a dense wall of trees fifteen minutes from the Community Center. How we made it this far, I don't know. I almost went down on him while he drove, but we're in the police's good graces right now and I didn't want to chance it.

When I told him what I was thinking, it opened the spout on *his* fantasies. I started tingling listening to him describe what he's going to do to me in the backseat of our rented wonder of precision German engineering.

Warm light spills through the sunroof and the windows. And I'm never letting this man go.

The humming turns throaty. "What did you say?"

"What?" I'm lost in the sensations caused by his roaming tongue.

"So we could leave?" Dan dances his fingers over the soft leather seat and smiles the same exact smile I see on his son when Bart's happily engaged in the moment. When he's creating something new and he knows his teacher has his back. That right now, he doesn't have to clean his cubby or pick up his paints.

He can enjoy being who he is.

"Only the truth," I say. Outside, the trees glisten and the world leaves us in peace. Which is what it needs to do, right now.

Dan hums again, his lips roaming across the upper edges of my bra's cups. "You still like me even though I'm dense?"

"You just need an education, Minion One."

"Yes, Ms. Frasier." Dan chuckles as he yanks down a cup, exposing a nipple. "I'll do everything you say, Ms. Frasier."

The way he suckles and flicks sends intense waves of pleasure through my breasts. The car is off and the cold is sneaking in, but my man has lit a fire in my soul.

And my body.

He moves against my pelvis, all hunched over in the back seat of the sedan in the cooling, turned-off-car air, rubbing his thigh against my still-covered pussy and humming against my frantically sensitive nipples.

"We have five days just for us?" I'm panting. I want to see his gorgeous chest and torso but I can't because we're in a car.

Dan yanks down the other cup of my bra and moves his efforts to my other breast. "Uh-huh."

"You took five days off? It's not going to be a problem?" Bart's in good hands, but I can't help worry about his business.

Dan looks up. An eyebrow pops up and his pirate smirk surfaces. "You worry too much."

"So we have five days of you doing *exactly* what you are doing right now?" No man has ever wanted to fuck me the way Dan does. It's not just sex. He wants to be close. To kiss.

To have his mouth on mine the same way it's on my nipples right now. His lips demanding all my attention while his fingers touch and stroke and express just how much he wants me.

Dan drops his mouth back to my nipple and hums his response.

Five days of loving this man.

"I will do *anything* you ask me to, Dan." I don't care what he wants. "I trust you more than I trust myself."

Dan comes up for air. "You're going to orgasm when I'm pounding you. It's going to be at the same time I come. I'm going to be in you and I'm going to see your beautiful eyes and feel your fingers in my hair. I'm going to feel your pussy tighten around my cock while I black out from the orgasm you give me because I love you."

No irony shows on his face. He's not playing. He's totally, completely serious.

"*Oh*..." I breathe. "We're going to do it in a way that makes both of us happy, aren't we?"

Dan's pirate smirk reappears. "Uh-huh."

When he returns his attention to my breasts, my back arches.

Because I love—and trust—this man to figure out what needs to be done.

And to do it right.

CHAPTER 25

Camille

"Mommy!" Bart walks carefully up the path from the dock toward the cabin's porch. He's wearing only his swim trunks, and a couple of mosquitos buzz around his head. His nose twitches like he wants to swat at them, but he's holding Isolde's—Isa, Rob calls her—big digital camera and he's doing a very nice job of not dropping it.

I set down my not-quite lemon-flavored water and swing my legs off the lounger. I think I'll stick to the non-flavored stuff but Sammie offered and I thought I'd try it. She's down on the dock with Tom, Rob, and Isa, talking about lighting over the lake and sunsets and appropriate amounts of art generation to write off our family vacation as work.

The steps creak when Bart takes them one at a time. "Smile!" he says when he crests the top one. The camera rises to his eye and he snaps a photo.

Part of me wonders why Isa is letting a five-year-old run around with one of her digital single lens reflex cameras, but the other part fully understands. My soon-to-be stepson's talents include all types of picture rendering. We've spent many weekends painting together, and working with photos in a couple of different editing programs.

"You're being careful with her camera?" I pat the lounger so he'll sit next to me. He's grown so much since his birthday I'm beginning to wonder if he'll be taller than me before he's out of elementary school. "Did you put on sunscreen?" I look over his young Norse King-slash-Highlander shoulders. "Don't get a sunburn."

"I did." Bart gives me one of his *Whatever, Mom* looks. "Stop worrying."

I chuckle and mess his hair. "Can't help that I love you."

Bart smiles and leans against my shoulder. "Uncle Robby and Isa want to go for a walk. Isa is bringing her other camera and she's going to show me how to take pictures the right way." He holds up the one strapped around his neck. "Uncle Tommy and Auntie Sammie are coming with. Can I go?"

I glance down at the dock. Sammie raises her water bottle and winks. She knows Dan and I haven't had a lot of alone time since we arrived on Wednesday night.

I wave a thank you.

"Sure. But put on a shirt and long pants, okay? And wear your sneakers. No flip flops on the trail." I rub his head again.

"Okay!" He kisses my cheek. "Thanks, Mommy."

I watch him carefully hold the camera as he wiggles through the screen door. From inside, I hear him tell his dad how he wants to take a picture of a moose.

Dan chuckles when he pushes through the door. He stops for a moment in the shade of the porch, his own water bottle in his hand, watching his brothers on the dock. "Rob's semi-girlfriend seems to have taken to Bart, even if they're still friend-zoning each other." He nods toward the water.

Isa leans her head toward Sammie and the sun glints off her blonde hair. I stand and lean against Dan and he hooks his thumb through the side of my bikini bottom.

"You took off the t-shirt." He's been wearing long-sleeved tees all weekend even though it's in the nineties, I think mostly because of

Rob's not-quite-girlfriend. But now I cuddle skin-to-skin against his broad chest.

"It's warm. No slush in the bones today." He shrugs. "Isa's nice."

I'm glad he feels comfortable enough to not worry about it. "She is. So are you." I kiss the edge of his sweep of chest hair. "Hot *and* sexy."

Dan takes a sip of his water. "Me or her?"

"Hmm." I glance at the dock. "Should I go blonde?" Could be fun.

Dan's eyes narrow. "Are there any Maori goddesses with pale hair?"

I chuckle. He's always looking for ways to get me worked up. Little scenarios. Ways to tempt me into using my imagination. We've developed quite a lot of coded looks and language. By the time we get Bart into bed, I'm usually ready to scream.

Once he figured out that's what I need, he's been unstoppable.

Sometimes I think he spends his bi-weekly sessions quizzing his therapist on conditioning techniques to use on me instead of taking the time to work on himself.

Same with his physical therapist.

Not that I'm complaining. He's happy and healthy. The man next to me is a joy to live with.

"So they're taking Bart for a walk, huh?" Another finger floats over my skin and into my bikini bottom.

"That's the plan."

"How long will they be gone?" He's watching the dock and I can tell he's holding in his pirate smirk.

Bart bounds out the screen door dressed appropriately for a walk, except his shoes are untied. The camera's strap loops around his neck, but it's twisted and doesn't look comfortable. "Taking pictures!" He holds up the camera.

"You be careful with that thing." Dan points his water bottle at Bart's chest.

Bart rolls his eyes. He stopped sticking his fists into his waist about a month ago and now makes faces instead. "Yes, Daddy."

"And tie your shoes." Dan points at Bart's feet.

Bart rolls his eyes again but bends carefully, maneuvering the camera around his knees, and ties his shoes. Then he's off, down the path, toward his uncles. They walk away along the lake's beach pebbles, two Quidell couples and their young nephew.

I like the lake. The cabin has been in the Quidell family since the fifties and has a quaint charm, though we'll need to build on as the family grows. The kitchen needs upgrading, anyway. "You and Tom talk about adding studio space?" The men spent a good deal of time discussing options yesterday.

Dan drops his water bottle on the lounger and scoops me up. My legs swing into the air and he lifts me over his shoulder in a firefighter's carry, and I screech like Bart when one of his uncles swings him around.

"That be a fine backside you have there, Ms. Frasier." His free hand works completely into my bottoms and he grips my ass with quite a lot of determination. "Think I'll pilfer it for me own."

Dan nibbles on my hip.

"Put me down." But I don't mean it. His shoulder feels rock hard against my breasts and I have a nice view of the muscular v of his lower back.

"Aye, matey." Dan swings open the door, twisting expertly to carry me in without knocking my head or knees or ass. "The waters be calm. And I do say I be tossin' a lovely maiden down on me bunk."

"Down. Oh God yes." I nibble on his shoulder blade and watch as Dan kicks his foot back, hooks the door to our bedroom, and slams it shut without turning around.

We're alone in our little room surrounded by suitcases and Bart's toys. It smells like the woods—moist and alive—and a cool breeze moves through the open windows. The plaid curtains rustle but the room's bright and cheery in the middle of the day.

"The massage oil is in my bag." I point at the floor, under the window.

Dan grunts and strips my bottoms off before he drops me onto our bed. The box spring groans and creaks and I bounce up, a good couple of inches of air between me and the bedding.

Twenty feet from the porch into the bedroom and he's already hard enough he's straining his cargo shorts.

"I think you fancy a roll in the sheets, my good sir." I reach for the zipper on his fly but he pushes me down on the bed, bending over me, a palm on each breast.

"I think you should wear your bikini instead of a wedding dress." Dan yanks the cups of my top to the side and immediately rolls first one nipple along his tongue, then the other. "The past two days watching you on the dock and in that lounger wearing only black triangles over my favorite parts has been murder, woman. My will power is at its end."

His kisses trail down my chest to the edge of my rib cage. When I breathe in, he licks my bellybutton.

"You going to tie me up with my bikini, pirate man? Revenge is yours."

Dan grunts again, frowning. His fingers make quick work of untying my top and he pulls it out, looking at the cups like he's got no idea what to do. "The straps are too flimsy." Frowning again, he props himself up on his elbows and fiddles with the top's ties. An eyebrow arches and he snorts. "Won't get enough force on the pressure points on your wrists. It'll bite into your skin and not do what it's supposed to do."

The pout on his handsome lips causes a full-body sigh from me. Dan's engineering-oriented brain produced some unexpected benefits and I have proof in our trove of "improved" toys.

Which I forgot to bring. But I have Dan. I pull him down on top of me. "Then to hell with it."

My top flies across the room.

I breathe in his ear. A shudder runs through his magnificent body.

"Take off the shorts, gorgeous," I whisper.

Dan grunts again. The fabric of his shorts rubs against my hips. I feel him work his way out of his boxers and hear the cotton wisp against the bedding as it drops to the floor.

"Give me what I want," I breathe.

He's not careful and damn, it feels *good*. Dan moves up along my body so he pounds against my clit. I pant, taking him deeply. He slams me hard, hunching against my body, and I slowly scoot upward on the mattress with each hit, into a patch of warm sunlight. Gold covers my eyes but I still see Dan. I see the clear joy in his eyes. And his love.

"I love you, Daniel Quidell." I feel his cock's rhythmic pulses inside me and I yelp when he crashes into me one last time, groaning.

Dan pulls us to the pillows. "I love you, too, Camille Frasier," he says, his lips on my ear.

We lay together in the warm summer air, both happy. Both in the moment.

And I will never have it any other way.

The Story continues
in book three, **Robert's Soul**

Bad boy graduate student Robert Quidell meets his match when his roommate's sister moves into their apartment....

ROBERT'S SOUL PREVIEW
CHAPTER ONE

Robert

"**A** stopwatch was used to measure the interval of perambulation through the pre-determined social interaction area..."

I rub my glove's scratchy palm over my face. It's fifteen degrees outside and the bus's heater is busted, but at least I had the ride to read journal articles about the culturally anthropological implications of leisurely walks.

I rub my face again. Who the hell uses the verb *perambulate*?

The bus takes the last corner before my stop. I grip the side of the seat as I attempt to counter the inevitable sway. The moment the bus stops and my boots hit the concrete, I'm scampering my ass through the bus fumes to the drafty but warm apartment.

The University bus drops off seven blocks from home. I could wait the fifteen minutes for the city bus. Or I could trot the sidewalks with a laptop and twenty-five pounds of textbooks on my back, toasty warm from the effort and fully deserving of the beer awaiting me in my fridge.

The better choice, I do believe.

I stuff the article into my backpack before yanking the flaps of my prize yellow-and-black-striped, pointy-tipped winter hat over my ears. When one has a gift-bearing, almost-five-year-old nephew, one must wear one's badge of uncle-hood with pride. Which I do. Every day. And will continue to do so, until spring comes and the wind chill goes away.

Some days I wonder if I should have chosen a graduate school in a warmer climate. But I like it here, even if the weather is too much like home. This university offers a fresh start.

The bus groans and shudders as it pulls up to my stop. I jog down the steps to the cold concrete, and breathe in the crisp night air. I'm already halfway up the block when the bus rumbles away.

The stop is on the very edge of the university property, just beyond two old and huge dorms. The energy of academia wanes out here, off campus. We all sleep away from the grand and imposing structures of the University, but we don't *live* here. We live in our labs and offices, in our buildings and student unions. The beds are for sleep and sex.

More sleep than sex, at least for me.

New city, new school. A new reputation of seriousness and depth. Yet my dates continue to find the wonders of my undergrad years on the internet. I'm fully aware that I'm a "bad boy." And that women have expectations for how I am to express my badness.

Sometimes social media has its... drawbacks.

Cold air dances over my lips, to my cheeks, and then onto my eyeballs. The chill makes the buildings and the streets look cleaner, as if I'm looking through blue ice at a dust-free world. All the moisture in the air froze out and nothing floats on the wind anymore. The world stopped being human-built and is a faery-land cleansed of all the grit and grime.

Or my corneas crystalized and I'm too fucking cold to realize it.

I stuff my hands into the pockets of my jacket. The cold makes me thirsty and I focus on my awaiting beer.

The books in my bag press the slab of my laptop against my back and I wish I didn't have to carry the entire contents of my PhD program every time I go into campus. Plus today, I'm also carrying the twenty-three student assignments I need to grade over the weekend.

The teaching assistant gig pays tuition and fees, and nets me enough to pay rent and to eat. It's fun, too. Most undergrads take Intro to Cultural Anthropology to fulfill distribution requirements, making it a class they choose, so we don't get a lot of whining. At least my section didn't last semester. On the other hand, Mack, my roommate, told me stories: A drug arrest his first semester, a student who plagiarized and got off because his daddy's a big shot lawyer, the creepy male student who stalked the woman who TA'ed before me.

On the road next to the sidewalk, a car drifts by, obviously looking for an address. My breath clouds the air and I feel a little warmer now that I'm moving, so I push my bumblebee hat back, to get a better look at the world around me.

A musical beat bounces down the street. I hear faint and distant laughter.

Mack said something about a party tonight. I'd declined his invite, citing the contents of my backpack as my reason.

But mostly I'm trying not to meet women at parties anymore.

A new life needs new ways of living. And I no longer want alcohol to be a factor in how women assess what I have to offer.

My phone chimes. I try not to have it out in the open while I walk because there've been a few snatch and grabs around campus. Last week, a woman got held up at knife-point. So I glance around before pulling it out.

I pull off my glove and sweep my finger across my phone to unlock the screen. *Left the party*. *Headache*, pops up.

Mack must have just left the party. I immediately glance around again because my brain thinks it might see him leave. Except the apartment is a block west and on the other side of the party house.

My sister stayed, appears.

I stare at the message for a moment. Sister?

Then I remember: The photographer.

Isolde

MY TWIN BROTHER ONCE ASKED ME WHAT I SEE WHEN I LOOK AT

the world. We were kids playing in the woods, me in front and Mack following, climbing over fallen logs and dancing around holes and hollows. The trees smelled summer fresh and the sunlight flickered over leaves and vines and our upturned faces.

Before I answered, I turned my face to the sky, my eyes closed. Warmth smoothed over my skin. Clean air tasted as good as the water from a cool, bubbling fountain. I stood perfectly still, a child with her toes in the moss and her twin brother an arm's length away, weak before the truth: I don't see the truth.

The world is so much more than my eyes telling me "Don't trip on that," or "Watch out for the spider!" I don't *see* because what's around me is much more beautiful than my sorry eyes can measure.

Which is why I take pictures.

I'm not an artist. I'm a scientist. I take readings with my lenses and I run analyses with my processing software. I can't resist digging in and uncovering the truth. The pull to know—to experience—is too powerful.

So when my dear twin brother tells me to put away my brand-spanking-new, ultra-high-resolution, megapixel camera phone and "enjoy the party" I tell him to go away.

He stands close because bad pop music thumps through the house and if his lips were more than a foot away I wouldn't be able to hear him. Which, when I think about it, might be preferable.

"Isa, come on." Mack pushes his wire-rims up his nose and gives me one of his narrow, one-eyebrow-cocked eye rolls. It's meant to convey annoyance but mostly it shows condescension.

"You better not give that look to your students or you're going to get a ton of bad evaluations." I poke at his nose with my camera phone. Winter semester started last week and the party is supposed to be some sort "welcome back from break" celebration.

His look changes to one of perplexity as he leans closer. "What?"

Now I roll my eyes, knowing full well my face looks identical to his. Same muscle pulls. Same eyebrow arch. Same dirty blue eyes under the same dirty blonde hair. At least on him, the "dirty" looks more like verdigris in his eyes and copper in his hair. It makes him handsome under his glasses. Under mine, I just look like every other semi-chubby boring chick with a phone in her hand.

My dear brother rubs his forehead and his fingers shadow his face. The party's lights are low, with most of the house's illumination coming from the multitude of twinkling fairy lights woven through banisters, stapled up along the house's crown molding, and thrown over the random fifties art hanging on the walls.

The house must have been built in the thirties. The rooms circle the central stairwell and are all separated by grand double doors. Leaded glass panels top all the windows. I need to get a few shots of the moonlight through the bevels before I go.

"Why don't you talk to someone?" Mack waves his beer bottle. It's the same random microbrew I'm drinking and the stuff smells like piss.

Mack takes a sip out of his bottle and makes a *this is gross* face. "It's not an undergrad party, you know. They're all adults. Some have jobs."

I know a few people here. I come and go from this part of the world, and right now I'm in town for three days before I'm off to Namibia for my next shoot. It's a big deal—I'm assisting one of the best photojournalists working in the field and every time I think about the gig my stomach does flip-flops. Which is why Mack dragged me to this party. To take my mind off business.

But for me, my upcoming shoot is as much graduate school as Mack's current road toward a PhD. He's in cultural anthropology. I'm documenting "the cultural" for the anthropologists and the magazines.

It was nice of him, though, to store my stuff on such short notice during the month I'll be gone. One should have a permanent address, even if one is permanently not at home.

I had my fill of our mother's house when her new boyfriend moved in. Codependency is not my cup of tea. I'd rather be out in the world falling victim to my need to see instead of locked down in California.

I don't know what Mack told his roommate, though. Mack says he's a first-year student in his department. Called him "the new kid" and said he's charming. His name's Rob or Bob or maybe Cob. I don't remember, but I do remember the slight tick moving across Mack's cheek with he said "charming."

The twitch means the same thing now as it did in high school and our undergraduate years: Stay away, sister. We've got a player on our hands.

Not that players pay attention to me. I'm not their type, with the glasses and the ubiquitous camera equipment and the general round-ness to my hips and breasts. I glance down at my chest. My knit top's a little tight and my chosen-for-comfort-while-traveling black skirt and tights show more of my roundness than I generally like. Half a month in the wilds of Africa might just be what I need to finish thinning out. I dropped thirty pounds the last time I was overseas.

Not that I need thinning, really. Sometimes I wonder why my brain still thinks these thoughts.

Mack rubs his forehead again.

I touch his arm, drawing his attention. "One's starting, isn't it?"

Migraines began for my brother less than a week after we turned thirteen. They were pretty bad in high school, and it took him vomiting in the nurse's office to get him to admit something was wrong. I dragged him home and made Mom sober up enough to take him to the doctor.

He's been on meds ever since. Once we got into college, the headaches lessened, and he's been doing well lately, but I can tell when one starts.

If he goes home now, takes a med, and sleeps, he'll be fine tomorrow.

He nods yes.

"Do you want me to walk with you back to the apartment?" The party house is about five blocks from Mack's place. I stowed my stuff this afternoon, taking the key he gave me, before he dragged me here to see old friends and introduce me to his new ones.

Except the roommate. Rob-Bob-Cob was off somewhere. Mack said studying.

Mack waves me off before setting his bad beer on a low table against a wall. "No use you leaving as well. You haven't seen your friends in ages." He nods toward the living room. "I'll walk my own sorry ass home. The fresh air will do me good. The headache will clear up before I get back to the apartment. I promise."

He waves at the party again. "Just be quiet when you come in, okay? If you find Rob passed out on the couch, don't poke him. He has bad breath."

I snicker. So the player has his flaws.

But I can't abandon my brother. "I don't need to stay."

Mack pinches the bridge of his nose. "You want to get some more shots with that wonder of digital precision, don't you?" He points at my camera phone. "I know you do."

I do. I'm as fascinated by the new and developing language of social media photography as I am by the wilds of the planet and the cultures of humanity. It's another property of the world that needs documenting, measuring, and analyzing.

Mack nods over his shoulder. "Lisa was asking about you. She's in the living room. Go say hi."

I squeeze his hand. "Are you sure?" We all went to the same college in our undergraduate days and Lisa also came to this university with Mack. It'd be nice to talk to her.

Mack squeezes back. "Promise me you'll be careful walking back to the apartment, okay? See if someone will walk with you."

I frown. I can handle myself. You need skills if you're going to do fieldwork.

Mack frowns back at me. "Please."

"Yes, Dad."

He chuckles, but stops when it obviously hurts.

"Text me the moment you get home." I pat his arm. "I want to make sure you're okay."

My poor twin brother nods one last time. He pulls out his phone, swiping at the screen, and the sudden blue haze lights up his face. He waves the device in my general direction and makes his way toward the door, leaving me to fend for myself in the cultural jungle of a grad student party....

The Story continues in book three, **Robert's Soul...**

THE WORLDS OF
KRIS AUSTEN RADCLIFFE

Hot Contemporary Romance:

The Quidell Brothers
Thomas's Muse
Daniel's Fire
Robert's Soul
Thomas's Need
Andrew's Kiss *(coming soon)*

Genre-bending Science Fiction about
love, family, and dragons:

WORLD ON FIRE
Series one
Fate Fire Shifter Dragon
Games of Fate
Flux of Skin
Fifth of Blood

Bonds Broken & Silent
All But Human
Men and Beasts
The Burning World

Series Two
Witch of the Midnight Blade
Call of the Dragonslayer (*coming soon*)

Smart Urban Fantasy:

Northern Creatures
Monster Born
Vampire Cursed
Elf Raised
Wolf Hunted (*coming soon*)

`

ABOUT THE AUTHOR

As a child, Kris took down a pack of hungry wolves with only a hard-cover copy of *The Dragonriders of Pern* and a sharpened toothbrush. That fateful day set her on a path traversing many storytelling worlds —dabbles in film and comic books, time as a talent agent and a text-book photo coordinator, and a foray into nonfiction. After co-authoring *Mind Shapes: Understanding the Differences in Thinking and Communication*, Kris returned to academia. But she craved narrative and a richly-textured world of Fates, Shifters, and Dragons—and unexpected, true love.

Kris lives in Minnesota with her husband, two daughters, Handsome Cat, and an entire menagerie of suburban wildlife bent on destroying her house. That battered-but-true copy of *Dragonriders*? She found it yesterday. It's time to pay a visit to the woodpeckers.

Fore more information
www.krisaustenradcliffe.com
krisradcliffe@sixtalonsign.com

www.ingramcontent.com/pod-product-compliance
Lightning Source LLC
Chambersburg PA
CBHW061137200626
46817CB00016B/1706